TEA FOR TWO, OR THREE?

Brenda Hawkins-Murray

MINERVA PRESS

LONDON
ATLANTA MONTREUX SYDNEY

TEA FOR TWO, OR THREE?
Copyright © Brenda Hawkins-Murray 1998

All Rights Reserved

ISBN 1 86106 912 X

First Published 1998 by
MINERVA PRESS
195 Knightsbridge
London SW7 1RE

Printed in Great Britain for Minerva Press

TEA FOR TWO, OR THREE?

Chapter One

It was the beginning of May 1940 when Jean realised why she was feeling so awful. She was pregnant. It couldn't be anything else. She'd felt exactly the same when she'd been expecting Jeff and Ken; lethargic, run down, tired, and off her food. That was all she needed. Most women usually had morning sickness when they were pregnant. Not Jean.

Jeffery was born in 1936 on 1st October, and was now three and half years old. He'd been a sickly child in his short life – first he'd contracted a form of paralysis that left one leg slightly shorter than the other, and then he'd developed asthma, leaving him with breathing problems. Fortunately he didn't have many asthma attacks, but when he did they were quite severe, and it was this that worried Jean. He had not had one for six months, so Jean kept her fingers crossed, hoping his attacks would ease off as he got older. He was thin and quite lanky, and if you didn't know any better you would think he was an underfed child, although he definitely was not. He ate like a horse. Despite all the problems he'd had, Jeff was a surprisingly healthy, happy and bright child.

Ken was only eighteen months old, and the complete opposite to Jeff. Born in September 1938, he was a chubby child and had always been healthy, although he always seemed to be grizzling. Anything seemed to make him cry. Jean just hoped he would grow out of it; sometimes she didn't know what to do about it. She had even taken him to the doctor to find out what caused it, but he had said that he couldn't find anything wrong. The doctor had said more or less what Jean had hoped – that he would probably grow out of it.

But why couldn't Tom have been more careful when he was home on leave last February? She had done her best, but once he got going he threw all caution to the wind.

What am I going to do? she asked herself. The war has only just started, and if this happens every time Tom's on leave... I only hope it's a short war like they're promising. Damn and blast!

Tom had been at summer camp with the Territorial Army when war had broken out. Instead of coming home after the camp, he was drafted into the regular army and sent for training. Two of his six brothers, Tom being the eldest, were with him on that summer camp and they stayed with him, and they were all in the Royal Artillery together.

They were sent to a Searchlight Battery in Hyde Park and they stayed there for a few months. At the beginning they were able to get home some weekends but then their leave was stopped for a time because the Germans had stepped up their night raids on Britain, and they were needed to man the searchlights.

She had not been to see the doctor yet but she knew that he would say, 'You should have been more careful, Mrs Drummond.' And that is exactly what he said when she saw him the next day.

'You know what a bad time you had with the last one. What was his name again?'

'Kenneth.'

'Kenneth, that's right. What does Tom have to say about it?'

'I don't know. I haven't told him yet. I was waiting for you to confirm it.'

'Yes, well, you are definitely pregnant, and I would say you are about three months gone. So it will be due early November. Get this prescription,' said Doctor Braithwaite, peering over his half-moon spectacles, 'and come and see me in a month's time.'

'Yes, thank you, Doctor. Goodbye.'

'Goodbye Mrs Drummond, see you next month then. Take care.'

All the time she was thinking, Why couldn't he have said I wasn't pregnant, the silly old fool. She really wasn't being fair to him. He was an old dear really and he had looked after the family since they had moved there just before Christmas of '36.

Jean walked home across the Recreation Grounds, commonly known by all as the Rec, to where Florrie was watching Jeff and Ken play with her son Michael in the sandpit.

She had met Florrie when she had first moved to Long Ditton through their two sons, Michael and Jeff. Michael was nine months older than Jeff, but it hadn't made any difference to the boys or the two women. Florrie and Jean seemed to hit it off straight away and became very good friends.

Florrie Hunter was thirty-two years old, four years older than Jean. She was not very tall, at about five foot two, with grey eyes and rich brown shoulder-length hair. She had a very animated face that would break out into a charming smile if the occasion arose, and that seemed to be quite often. She had a marvellous sense of humour and was a very good friend to Jean. Whereas Jean was basically very shy, Florrie was very outgoing and would tell people to go to the devil if they had upset her. If she had been over-charged in a shop she would tell the shopkeeper loudly, in front of whoever else was in the shop that he had done so, just in case the same thing happened to them.

God forbid if anyone had upset any of her friends, especially Jean; she would go to any length to defend them. A lot of people who knew her only slightly thought she was a rather bossy person. She definitely was not. She had a heart of gold. Generous to a fault, she would give her last penny if she thought it would help you.

'What did he say?' asked Florrie when Jean arrived. She did not need to wait for an answer as she could tell by Jean's face what the answer was. 'What are you going to do now?'

'I haven't a bloody clue, Florrie! Just go ahead and tell Tom I suppose. God knows what he'll say.'

Things must have been bad for Jean to have sworn. That was the first time she had ever heard her swear in all the time she had known her. Tom has a lot to answer for, getting Jean pregnant again so soon after her having Ken, and on their small income.

'Do you really want this baby?' asked Florrie.

'Of course not. What can I do about it?'

'Well you could er, um—'

'Oh no! I couldn't do that,' said Jean, horrified to think where Florrie's thoughts were leading. 'Definitely not. Anyway, I can't afford that.'

Florrie burst out laughing. 'You should have seen your face just then. I didn't mean an abortion as such.' Florrie lowered her voice on the word 'abortion'.

'Phew! You had me worried then. I can just see me going to a back street old hag with dirty fingernails to have it done.' Jean shuddered at the thought. 'Anyway, are there any around here? This area doesn't strike me as having those sort of places.'

'Of course not! At least, not that I know of. That's not what I meant,' still laughing at Jean's expression.

'Then what did you mean?'

'I meant that old wives' tale about gin and hot baths.'

'I can't stand gin, it tastes like... sssh,' said Jean looking up to see the boys coming their way. Jeff and Michael were running, and poor Ken was toddling behind them trying to keep up.

As usual Ken was grizzling. Jeff was rubbing his hands and brushing sand from his trousers and Michael was laughing at something Jeff had said.

Jean pulled Ken toward her, gave him a kiss and a cuddle and wiped his eyes and nose with her hanky.

'What is the matter dear?' said Jean looking concerned.

'Me too. Me too,' demanded Jeff holding out his arms to Jean. Jean smiled lovingly at Jeff and pulled him to her, kissed and cuddled him too, and blew raspberries on his cheeks, causing Jeff to giggle.

Florrie watched them and smiled, but was still thinking that Tom should have been more careful. Instead, to lighten the mood she said, 'Come on. No more tears. Who wants to come to Aunty Florrie's for tea then?'

The three boys were jumping up and down. Even Ken wiped his tears away with the back of his hands and was now smiling.

Both Jeff and Ken loved going over to Florrie's, and whenever they got the opportunity they were over there like a shot.

'Florrie,' Jean said in exasperation, 'we were over there on Tuesday. You and Michael come to my place, please. We've to go through it to get to yours.'

'No. Come on boys. We have to be democratic over this. What do you want to do?' she asked. Turning to Jeff and Ken she asked, 'My home with Michael or your place?'

'Come to you Aunty Florrie please,' said Jeff.

'Then it's settled. Come on let's get off home and put the kettle on.'

Jean lifted her eyebrows heavenward and Florrie gave her a smile and a wink, then turned and walked ahead, holding Michael and Jeff's hands whilst Jean followed behind with Ken in her arms.

Chapter Two

Florrie's house, a cottage, really, was the carbon copy of Jean's and backed onto Jean's. Jean's fronted onto the main Portsmouth Road and Florrie's fronted onto the River Thames.

They were a pretty basic, two up and two down, with a toilet in the back yard. There was no garden, just the concrete back yard for the children to play in, with a high fence on the three sides. In the fence that divided Jean's place from Florrie's Joe and Tom had made a gate so that the children and Jean and Florrie could go back and forth and the children could play somewhere safe. It was a good idea.

Arriving at home Jean opened the front door and they all trooped through to the gate in the fence to Florrie's place.

'Is there anything I can do?' Jean asked.

'Yes please – will you put the kettle on and make the tea? Now let's see what we have in here to eat for tea,' said Florrie as she stood on a chair and rummaged around in the cupboard that was too high for her to reach from the floor. It was where she kept her stock of tinned food. She had always believed in having a good stock cupboard.

She brought out a pre-war tin of ham. Jean noticed and said, 'Oh no Florrie, we can't possibly eat that. Save it for a special occasion or for when Joe comes home on leave.'

'I have another two tins in there. Anyway, this is a special occasion, sort of.'

Jean reluctantly agreed with Florrie. A special occasion this was, but not the sort that she felt like celebrating.

She heaved a sigh and got up to make the tea as the kettle had just boiled.

'Come on, cheer up Jean. It could be worse.'

Jean put the teapot on a table mat, shooed the cat off the table and started getting cups and saucers, and mugs for the boys, from the dresser.

The boys were playing in the back yard and making a hell of a lot of noise. Florrie went to the back door and called them in.

'Come on lads, let's be having you then. Wash your hands before sitting down.'

The boys trotted in obediently and washed their hands as best they could by taking it in turns standing on a chair at the kitchen sink. Jean had to help Ken.

Jean sat back down and watched them. Being old cottages they were small, and there was no room for a bathroom, not that either Florrie or Jean had ever lived in a house with a bathroom. The bath was hanging on a nail in the back yard wall. Everyone called it a Tin Lizzie. It was galvanised so that it would not go rusty and was got in once a week for bath nights, usually Fridays.

When you came in the front door you stepped straight into what was called the front room, living room or front parlour, depending on where you were brought up. Both Jean and Florrie called it the front room. Only people with ideas of grandeur called it a front parlour. Up two steps was the kitchen-dining room. Actually it was an all-purpose room. Jean and Florrie spent all their spare time in the kitchen as it was a lot cosier than the front room, especially in the winter.

Jean was brought out of her reverie by Ken starting to grizzle again.

'What is wrong now Ken?' Patiently Jean wiped his nose and eyes yet again and watched as Ken rubbed his left ear.

'Hurt, Mummy. Ear hurts.'

'Let Mummy look at it.' Jean lifted him onto her lap and peered into his ear. It looked an angry red.

'I've still got some of that stuff left from when Michael had a bad ear. Doc Braithwaite dishes it out left right and centre for bad ears. Do you want me to get it?'

'Oh yes please, Florrie dear. I know the stuff you mean. I've got some of that in my place too, from when Jeff had an earache.'

'We'll use mine for now and we'll use yours next time. Meanwhile you can pour the tea while I go and find it.'

Jean poured tea for them both and gave some milk to the three boys. Ken was still grizzling and she felt sorry for him. She just hoped that the ointment worked on Ken's ear as she didn't fancy going back to see Doctor Braithwaite so soon.

Florrie came back with the ointment and proceeded to treat Ken's ear. After putting a drop of the warmed ointment in his ear she finished off by putting a small piece of cotton wool in.

'Beautifully done, Nurse Florrie! I couldn't have done better myself. Thank you,' said Jean.

'I don't know what is in that stuff but whatever it is, it works wonders. Now for that cup of tea.'

They sat quietly for a time, each with her own thoughts until Florrie broke the silence by asking Jean,

'What do you think of my suggestion of this afternoon. Have you thought any more about it?'

'Well I have...'

'But?'

'But what about the regulation three inches of bath water. That wouldn't do much good!'

'True. But I won't tell if you won't,' laughed Florrie.

'Of course I won't. But what about the gin side of it?' said Jean also laughing.

'Well, we could start tonight when we go to pay the Club money.'

'Okay. But I am not relishing it. You know I can't even stand gin. Isn't there another spirit that tastes more pleasant?' asked Jean hopefully.

'I don't really know. I've only heard of the gin for this sort of thing.'

'I suppose it will have to be gin then. Yuk!'

'Yuk. Yuk. Yuk,' said the boys in chorus picking up on what Jean had said.

'Sssh. Get on with your tea,' demanded Jean.

They laughed. Even Ken did. The pain in his ear must be easing off. Thank heavens, Jean thought.

'Come on Jeff, Ken. If you have finished we'd better get you home to bed. Thank Aunty Florrie for the nice tea.' To Florrie she said, 'I'll be back to help you clear up, then we'll go and pay the Club money in if you like.'

'No need to help me clear up, there isn't much mess. I'll see you at about eight o'clock.'

'All right then. And thanks for the smashing tea. See you about eight. I just hope there isn't an air raid tonight.'

Florrie watched her friend go out the back door and go through the gate in the fence waving to Jean who waved back. Poor Jean, she thought. I just hope the gin and hot baths work.

Chapter Three

They liked to go and pay the Club money on a Friday night. It was their one treat of the week that they really looked forward to. They paid it in at the City Arms, a little pub at one end of the cottages. At the opposite end was a coal merchant's yard. There were only twelve cottages so it wasn't far to the pub. In fact there was only one other cottage between both Jean's and Florrie's. Mrs Mitchell always listened out for the children and would come and tell Jean or Florrie if anything was up.

The City Arms was divided into two bars, the Lounge and the Public Bar. Florrie and Jean always went in the Lounge bar as it was a bit quieter and nicer in there. Florrie ordered a gin and lemonade for Jean and a schooner of sweet sherry for herself. The Landlord said, 'Good evening ladies. And how are you both?'

'Fine thank you, and yourself and Mrs Blake?'

'We're both well thanks. Having a celebration are we?'

'Not really. Jean just fancied a change. Didn't you luv!'

'Yes,' she said, blushing at the untruth Florrie had told Jack.

Florrie came and sat down smiling at Jean's discomfort. 'Well, I had to say something didn't I?'

'I suppose so,' agreed Jean reluctantly.

'I could have said, "No, Jean is pregnant and she wanted a drop of mothers ruin to try and get rid of it", couldn't I?' Jean laughed and she took a sip of the gin. 'Say, this isn't too bad with lemonade. Cheers.' She tapped her glass to

Florrie's in salute. Jack called across to them and asked if they were paying any Club money that evening. When they answered that they were, he said he'd tell Alan when he came in. Jean blushed again. Florrie noticed and said, 'What is it with you and Alan Armstrong? Is it something I should know about?'

'Of course not. What are you talking about anyway?'

'You and Alan!'

Jean insisted there was nothing for Florrie to get suspicious about. That made Florrie raise her eyebrows at the vehemence that was in Jean's voice. It was true there was nothing for Florrie to be suspicious about. She and Alan only saw each other in the City Arms, in full view of everyone: there was absolutely nothing going on between them, but Jean had often wondered what it would be like to be kissed by him. Alan Armstrong was a very handsome man, about thirty years old standing 6' 2" in his bare feet. He had very dark brown eyes, which in some lights looked more black than brown, like his hair, which was black too. He had strong broad shoulders that went down to a narrow waist. Jean only assumed that the rest of his body, which she couldn't see, was in as marvellous a condition. The broad shoulders probably came from playing rugby for Cambridge University when he was there a few years ago, and lately for a local club. Alan worked in aircraft design, for Armstrong Siddeley in Kingston. That was where he usually worked, but lately he had been working at the Perspex factory down the road, which was a subsidiary of the Kingston plant.

'I must admit that he has rather dreamy eyes though,' said Jean wistfully.

'Is there something you should be telling me?' Florrie asked.

'No, but...' Florrie leaned closer to Jean, 'but I wish there was. He is rather gorgeous isn't he?'

'Jean!' Florrie exclaimed. From the shock in her expression Jean could see that she had upset her friend.

'Oh no, Florrie. It is only wishful thinking. Only kidding. You know how much I love Tom. And you know I would never do anything to hurt him. It's just a dream after all. Don't you ever have fanciful dreams?' At that moment Alan Armstrong walked into the lounge from the bar so Florrie was unable to answer.

'Hello Jean,' said Alan, turning on one of his most charming smiles for her benefit, and then turned said, 'Hello Florrie. How is it going with Tom and Joe away?' He said the last looking at Jean. Florrie jumped in before Jean could say anything and said, 'We are both fine and managing quite well really, thank you Alan. How are things with you? Still working at the Perspex factory?'

'Yes I am, but I'd be in the forces doing my bit for King and Country if I had my way. Being in a reserved occupation I can't join, more's the pity.'

'Which Service would you go in if you had the choice and were free to join?' asked Jean.

'The Royal Navy.'

'I can just see you in one of those jaunty hats and bell-bottomed trousers,' said Jean laughing. Alan laughed too, then asked them how much they wanted to pay into the club this week. Jean said two shillings and Florrie said two and six.

'That's fine,' said Alan entering the amounts into their books. The idea was to pay in what you could afford towards your Christmas savings, which in Florrie and Jean's case was not much. It was nice at Christmas time to have a little extra to buy presents for their families and some extras for the Christmas dinner, though that depended on what they could buy with their Ration Books. Alan looked up as he gave them their club books back and caught Jean watching him. She looked away from him.

Alan's heart gave a lurch. Jean was a very beautiful woman, and if she hadn't been married to Tom he would have been there to ask her out and get to know her better. But she was married to Tom, so it was no use wishing. In the ensuing silence he said, 'Did you know that I am your local Air-Raid Warden?'

'No,' both Florrie and Jean answered.

'Well I am, so I'll be around to check your blackout arrangements,' he said with a smile.

'I can assure you that our arrangements are fine, thank you Alan. Jean made all our blackout curtains. And Joe stuck brown paper tape across all our windows and Jean's too.' Jean looked across to Florrie and asked her if she would like another drink. Alan said he would buy them.

'No thanks,' said Jean. 'I'm drinking gin, and you know the price of that these days.'

Alan said that it didn't matter, he was going to buy them one and with that picked up their glasses and proceeded to the bar. Sniffing Florrie's schooner he asked, 'Is that sweet or dry sherry Florrie?'

'Sweet please, Alan.' He ordered the drinks and brought them over, saying that he must love them and leave them as he had some more collections to do.

'I'll probably see you later.'

'Okay, and thanks for the drinks,' said Jean.

Alan said it was his pleasure and Florrie mumbled under her breath, 'Yeah. I bet.' Fortunately Alan did not hear her, but if he did he didn't let on. Jean just laughed and said, 'You're jealous, Florrie Hunter!'

'I am not. I was just thinking of you. You know how he always spends a longer time with us than he should. I am just being practical. You know what they are like around here. One sneeze from you and it's all round Long Ditton in a flash that Jean Drummond has galloping pneumonia.'

'Oh Florrie,' said Jean laughing, 'you are a case! I have told you a million times not to exaggerate.'

'I know. But I am only thinking of you. I don't want you to get hurt. You know how bitchy the women are around here.'

'That's true. Look at Mrs Gregory down the Bridge. Someone told her husband, anonymously, that a chap kept staying there overnight. And all the time it was her brother. You see what I mean?'

'Yes I do. I have no intention of going astray, with Alan or anyone else,' Jean said. 'I love Tom too much.'

'They can be had up for that sort of thing. Isn't it libel or slander?'

'It depends whether it is written or spoken. But I'm not sure which is which. Anyway, it certainly set the cat amongst the pigeons with the Gregorys. He was really mad when he last came home on leave and confronted her with it. I bet he'd love to know who wrote the note.'

'Yes, I am sure he would,' Florrie said, 'and this my young friend is getting us nowhere nearer to a solution to your problems. Come drink up and let's have another one.'

Jean got up to get the drinks and said that this would have to be the last for her tonight as she felt that the gin was making her a bit merry. Even Florrie had been giggling more than usual.

'Yes, we had better get back soon to see how the boys are.' And with that the two friends downed their drinks and walked the fifty-odd yards home. They kissed goodnight and each went to her own cottage.

Chapter Four

Jean did not feel tired or tipsy anymore. The short walk in the fresh air must have woken her up. She went up to the boys' room and walked over to see how Ken was. He had thrown the blankets off as usual but apart from that he was sleeping peacefully. She was pleased to see that his ear did not appear to be playing up.

Jeff was sleeping peacefully as well, and it looked as though he had not turned over at all since he went to bed. He was a funny little mite, thought Jean. Always so particular about his hands. He had a fetish keeping them clean, which was strange really in one so young, especially a little boy.

Jean had a lick and a promise at the kitchen sink, tidied up the few toys that were on the floor and went up to her lonely empty bed.

Things went on much as usual. The gin and the earlier hot baths had not worked, so that was a waste of money for the gin, and water for the baths. Jean now resigned herself to telling Tom.

She was four and a half months along the way, so it was dangerous to try any more tricks. Naturally she was disappointed but she had come to accept it. She got out the writing paper and envelopes and started a letter to Tom. She told him that she was expecting the baby in November and asked if he would be able to get home for it.

She went across to Florrie's to ask her if she would watch the boys for her.

'I want to catch the last post,' she said, waving the letter in the air.

'Pop in for a cuppa when you get back, Jean.'

'Okay. Bye.' She dashed through the back door and out the front door and made her way to the post office for a stamp, posted the letter and turned around in a bit of a hurry, bumping straight into Alan.

'Where's the fire?' he said.

'Oh, I am so sorry! Are you all right?'

'More to the point, are you?'

'Yes I'm okay. I just wasn't looking where I was going. I was just trying to catch the last post with a letter to Tom,' said Jean breathlessly.

'How is Tom? It seems ages since I have seen him.'

'I haven't seen him since February. I don't even know where he is, just some postal address in London. At least he is still in this country.'

'How can you be so sure of that in times likes these?'

'He would have been home on embarkation leave if the Army was going to ship him overseas.'

'Of course. I'd forgotten that. Anyway how's about coming with me to Ma Raymond's for a cup of tea?'

'No thank you. I've promised Florrie I'd go there for a cup. Thanks all the same Alan. Perhaps another time.'

'Another time,' said Alan, rather disappointed.

'Goodbye Jean. See you Friday down the City Arms.'

'Goodbye Alan. Yes, I'll see you Friday.' Jean hurried on home.

When she reached Florrie's the boys were sitting eating biscuits and sipping home-made lemonade. Florrie poured the tea and cut Jean a piece of cake.

'Florrie, I don't want a piece of cake thank you. You must save it for Michael.' Jean knew that that was probably Florrie's egg and sugar ration for the week that had been used in the cake. That was why she would not have any, despite having bought a pint of milk for the tea on the way over.

'Nonsense. I won't take no for an answer,' said Florrie putting a big chunk on a plate for her. 'You need fattening up, in any case. So "Hush yo' mouff, Miz Scarlett",' laughed Florrie in poor imitation of Mammy from the book *Gone with the Wind*.

Jean laughed with her. 'I don't know what I'd have done without you these past few weeks, Florrie. You've kept me sane.' Jean smiled at Florrie and said, 'Thank you.'

'What are friends for if not to help?'

'You've done more than your fair share of it and I can't thank you enough. Is there anything that you want that I can give you or do for you?'

'Well let me see,' said Florrie thinking. 'Of course not, silly. So shut up and drink your tea.'

They sat in companionable silence sipping their tea until Florrie broke the silence by saying, 'There is something you can do if you really must.'

'What's that? Anything, you know that.'

'Do you remember that dress that I bought in Kingston before the war? You know, that one with a pale blue background with white flowers on it?'

'Oh yes,' said Jean, 'it was lovely, but slightly tight across the hips, as far as I can remember, but you said, "I'll go on a diet." Does it fit now?'

'Of course not. I'd have thought with this food rationing I could have lost pounds. But no. Not even an ounce. Anyway, could you make it into a blouse for me?'

'I don't see why not, it should be easy enough unless you want it completely remodelled,' said Jean. 'Go and get it and I'll have a look at it.'

Florrie went up the stairs to her bedroom while Jean gazed out of the window at the three boys. Michael was playing at being an aeroplane with his arms spread out for the wings and going 'Brrrrrrr, Brrrrrrr,' in imitation of the noise they made. He said, 'I'm dropping a bomb.' It was followed by one hell of a crash as Jeff lifted up the metal dustbin lid and threw it as high as he could. Ken burst out crying with fright and came running in to Jean.

Jean smiled and called out of the window to tell Jeff and Michael to keep the noise down.

Florrie returned clutching the dress and said, 'What was all that row about? It made me jump'.

'Only Jeff and Michael playing at aeroplanes. Jeff threw the dustbin lid up in the air. That's what all the row was,' laughed Jean and added, 'the little beggars.'

The boys were playing a bit quieter now as Florrie said, 'I'll give them what for if I catch them playing war games. Don't they have enough with the real thing?' Florrie asked.

'Boys will be boys, as they say. I wonder what bright spark thought that saying up.'

'Probably one who has no children, and sits all day in an ivory tower making up stupid quotations thinking they are clever. The quotations, not the person.'

They both laughed at Florrie's assumption and Jean poured another cup of tea with great care as Ken was still on her lap.

'Now then. Let me have a look at that dress,' said Jean, holding out her arms for it. Ken had already eased down from Jean's lap and had gone out to the back yard again. It was a bit quieter out there so he was not so scared.

'It won't be any trouble to make it into a blouse,' said Jean frowning slightly. 'Do you know what I could do? I could let out all the darts, and even the seams in the skirt of the dress and you will have a dress that looks like new and is beautiful again. What do you say?'

'Are you sure it won't be too much trouble to do that?'

'Of course not. It will be easier than making it into a blouse. But if you still want a blouse I will do it for you.'

'If you can let the seams out I would rather keep it as a dress.'

Jean said, 'That's settled then. Go and try it on and I will pop over and get some pins.'

When Jean went out in the back yard the boys were playing with some marbles that belonged to Michael.

Jean came back with the pins and started clearing the tea things from the table and wiping the surface. Florrie came in wearing the dress.

Jean looked at it and said, 'Mmm. I don't think I'll have to do anything with the bodice except let out the bottom darts at the waistband. The seams have plenty of material left in them, and there is a lot spare in the gathers of the skirt for me to let out easily. You can tell this is a pre-war dress by the amount of material spare in it. It is a pity I never thought of altering it before for you.'

'That's okay. At least I'll be able to wear it at last instead of it taking up space in the wardrobe.'

'What's today?' asked Jean.

'Wednesday. Why?'

'Why? If I start on your dress tonight I will have finished it by Friday and you will be able to wear it when we go to pay the Club money in.'

'Great. You go and get started and I will look after the boys and keep them out of your hair.'

Jean took the dress and left the boys in Florrie's very capable hands.

She liked dressmaking and all aspects of it. And she was very good at it too.

Before she was married she worked as a seamstress for a firm in Knightsbridge. When she had finished her training, she was a fully-fledged court dressmaker. The firm had a Royal Charter so Jean was often working on beautiful dresses and gowns for Lady This and Lady That, and sometimes even Duchesses, though she'd never worked on anything the Royal Family wore. That work was always reserved for the boss and her assistant.

She really enjoyed the work there and was sorry when she left and was married. Tom did not believe in his wife working. He was old-fashioned in that way. But Jean accepted it, for that was the way things were done then.

I wonder what Tom makes of the women at work now, thought Jean. Married women, and working at such unwomanly things like in munitions factories and in the Armed Forces too.

There was no doubt about it, she definitely missed working at something she knew she was good at. At least she didn't have to buy any clothing. Anything that could be made of fabric, cotton, silk, wool or velvet, Jean could make it. It was a pity there was not much fabric available these days. You needed so many clothing coupons to get material enough to make anything with.

So she was pleased to do this little favour for Florrie. The fact was, she rather enjoyed working on the dress, and for Jean it was so easy to do.

Chapter Five

The dress was ready by Friday so Florrie was able to wear it to the City Arms. She looked very pretty in it and was pleased that she had thought of it.

When Jack the landlord saw them he whistled and said Florrie looked 'real elegant'.

Lil, Jack's wife, came through from the bar to see who Jack was whistling at.

'My oh my! What a pretty frock,' Lil said. 'Is it new?'

'No,' said Florrie. 'Jean did it over for me by letting it out. Didn't she do a good job? Jean used to be a court dressmaker you know.'

'Well I never. I didn't know that. Could you do some of my dresses for me please, Mrs Drummond?'

'It's Jean. Call me Jean. And yes, if the dresses are pre-war for they have more spare material in the seams than they do nowadays,' volunteered Jean.

'Would you really? Of course I'll pay you for your trouble.'

'No, I co—' she was about to say that she couldn't take any money when Florrie dug her in the ribs and asked Jack for 'Two schooners of sweet sherry, please Jack.'

Lil turned to Jack and said, 'On the house, Jack luv.'

'How kind of you,' simpered Florrie, fluttering her eyelashes at Jack.

Jean took the drinks, trying not spill them; she was shaking with laughter and she just had to turn her back to the people at the bar.

'What's wrong with you Jean?'

'You, you fool.' And Jean couldn't restrain her laughter any longer and she just let it rip.

Florrie put her hands on her chest and said with as much indignation that she could muster, 'Me? Me? What do you mean by saying "me"?' She was all innocence.

'Oh shut up and drink your drink,' said Jean, still laughing. 'You know exactly what I mean.'

'Well. Really. You could have thrown up a chance of making some money, and Lil must have plenty of dresses that need letting out.'

'That's not all I could have thrown up. It was you making obvious eyes at Jack that set me off. Now let's drop it,' Jean said still shaking a little with mirth. Florrie was laughing too, and Alan chose that moment to walk in.

He walked up to them smiling and asked, 'What is it that has tickled your fancies, ladies?' That only set them off again and there were tears running down their faces.

'Nothing,' Florrie managed to say.

'It must have been something,' insisted Alan.

But they were saved from answering by the air-raid siren going off. That had a sobering effect on all of them.

Both Jean and Florrie ran to door followed by Alan who said, 'I'll give you a hand with one of the boys if you like, Jean.'

'Yes thanks. Will you be all right Florrie? I'll meet you back in the shelter.'

'Okay,' called Florrie.

Jean dashed round to her cottage, let herself in with Alan close on her heels. They got to the bedroom just as Jeff and Ken were beginning to cry with fear. The siren made an awful sound which was like all the banshees in hell wailing.

Alan grabbed Jeff, who was nearest the door, and held the door open while Jean, with Ken in her arms, brushed past him. As she did so, her breast accidentally rubbed up against his arm. The shock of the unexpected contact sent a thrill right through Jean. It was exquisite. Not stopping, she said, 'We'd better hurry.' Why did I say that? she thought. We are hurrying.

They dashed outside and back to the pub car park where the air-raid shelter was and went down the steps with the boys.

Florrie was already there, Michael sitting sleepily beside her. She held up her arms for Ken and said to Jean, 'Are you going back home now?'

'You can't do that! The siren has finished,' said Alan.

'Oh yes I can. I can't stand closed in spaces,' Jean looked around the air-raid shelter and shivered as if to prove her case and said, 'I'll see you when the raid is over. I'm going home.'

Alan turned with Jean and said, 'I'd better report in so I'll see that Jean gets home safely, Florrie.'

'See you later Jean. And thanks Alan.'

Jean and Alan ran around to Jean's cottage and just as they got there there was an almighty bang – then silence.

'Quick,' said Alan, pushing Jean through her front door. Then the evening was ripped by a terribly bright light and another crash of sound. With the light, Alan had seen the Morrison shelter in Jean's front room and pushed her down into it.

Again there was another loud bang and this time it blew the front window in. Alan threw himself over Jean to protect her from the glass. He lay like that until all the banging had finished and the glass had stopped falling. Fortunately no glass had got as far as the Morrison shelter. The brown paper strips stopped a lot of it. Jean could feel his weight on top of her. She was shocked at herself because of the thoughts going around in her head. And she rather liked the pressure. She felt safe with Alan there.

'Sorry Jean.'

'That's okay. And thanks.'

The blackout curtain had fallen down, letting in a bit of light. Alan looked down into Jean's eyes looking back at him. He couldn't help it. He leant down and kissed her fully on the lips.

She didn't do anything at first but she gradually put her hands to the back of his neck and pulled him closer. If she had been standing, her legs would have been weak and given way. As it was she was lying in her Morrison shelter bed with someone who wasn't her husband. She refused to let it worry her.

As Jean had put her arms around Alan he carried on kissing her. His lips moved down to her neck then to the slight opening where her breasts were just peeping above the V of her blouse.

Jean could feel all this as if in a dream, and suddenly reality set in and she started to push Alan away. But another explosion rattled the house and she clung even harder to him. 'Oh Alan! I am scared.'

'It's all right Jean. I'll stay here with you.' Jean visibly relaxed and Alan held her even closer.

He started to kiss her again, gently at first then getting more bold when she didn't object. She was enjoying the sensation. It had been nearly six months since Tom had been home, and she was only human. She could feel his hardness as Alan held her and she pushed herself up towards him. He buried his face in her breast then proceeded to run his hand up and down her bare leg, getting higher with each movement, and at last he reached the top of her leg where her panties covered her most private, and at that moment, very sensitive parts. His hand fluttered to a stop at her panties and started to ask Jean if he could continue, but for an answer Jean kissed him harder and started to undo the buttons of his shirt.

With that, Alan pulled Jean into a sitting position as best as he could with the low headroom, and started to undress her gently. She said, 'What about reporting for duty?'

'I have to protect a maiden in distress. And you are in distress aren't you?'

'Oh yes, kind sir.'

He stopped her with a kiss before she could say any more and continued to undress her. When he had taken the last of her clothes off he sat back on his heels and studied her in the moonlight that was coming in through the broken window.

'God you are beautiful.'

'Ssh,' said Jean reaching up to caress his chest. A sob escaped Alan's throat as he buried his face in her bare breast once again. His hand started to caress her left breast, flickering over the nipple, just about touching then flitting away before he made contact. Jean was going mad with desire, wanting him to do more.

As if reading her mind Alan gently put his mouth over her nipple and started sucking the left one, then the right one. By this time Jean's nipples were very erect and Alan continued to suck them, drawing his mouth and tongue over the large, desirable nipples. All the time he was caressing her breast, his right hand was caressing her legs. He slid his hand very gently toward the V of her legs and gently probed until he felt the moisture. She could feel his fingers down there and she shuddered and opened her legs. Alan took this as permission to proceed and he pushed his fingers into her. Further and further he went until his fingers could go no further. He quickly put his head down and started licking and kissing Jean on her stomach getting gradually lower. His tongue reached where his fingers were just a few seconds before and he started to probe with his tongue. Jean squirmed beneath him with desire. Suddenly Alan pushed himself up and entered her, slowly at first then faster and faster, in and out, in and out. It was all over in a few minutes, each of them reaching a shuddering climax at the same time.

Jean was about to speak but Alan silenced her with a soft kiss. He said, 'Jean I am so sorry. I don't know what came over me. But I have loved you since the first time I met you.'

'Don't reproach yourself. It was as much my fault as yours.'

Alan kissed her yet again and they proceeded making love again, this time much more slowly.

The sounds of bombs falling had gradually faded into the background. Jean and Alan wouldn't have heard them in any case for they were so wrapped up in what they were doing.

They must have dozed for they were rudely awakened by the all-clear going.

Jean sat up in a panic but Alan calmed her down and said, 'Get dressed and go and get the boys. I'll see you later.'

Jean rummaged round the scene of their lovemaking but could only find her skirt and blouse. It will have to do, she thought as she dashed for the front door. She realised that Alan must be a quick dresser – he had already gone.

Chapter Six

Jean rushed around to the air-raid shelter just in time to see the people pouring out. She felt so guilty for what she had just done, but she could not help it now. It was over and done with and would never happen again.

Florrie was carrying Ken and holding Jeff's hand and Mrs Mitchell was holding Michael's hand. Florrie saw Jean and nearly dropped Ken, she was so pleased to see that Jean was okay. She gave Jean a hug, nearly suffocating Ken.

'Oh Jean! I was so scared for you when I heard all the noise. I thought you were a goner.'

'I thought I was too. My front windows are out and the blackout curtain is down. But I don't know what else has happened as it is too dark to see. It seemed like forever that the raid went on. There's broken glass all over the front room. Thank God Tom insisted that we had the Morrison shelter installed.' Jean knew she was rambling but she was so thankful that the boys and Florrie were safe.

'We won't be able to see the extent of the damage until it gets light. What happened to Alan?' asked Florrie.

This is what Jean had been dreading but she lied and said, 'He dashed off before the first big bang. I was sitting there under the Morrison scared stiff and wondering if I will ever see you again. But I was too scared to come back out to the shelter.' Thank the Lord it was still dark so Florrie could not see her blushes as she lied.

Alan turned up then and said, 'Are you all right Jean? When I came past your place and saw that your windows had blown in well... Are you okay Florrie? Here, let me take Kenny from you.'

'I was huddled under the Morrison scared stiff at all the noise,' said Jean. 'What has happened?'

'A direct hit on the Village Hall. Thank God there was no one in it. And I think one bomb dropped on one of the Water Board's filter-beds.' Alan had gleaned all this from one of the other Wardens so he could pass it off as if he had been doing his duty.

'I'll give you a hand to get the boys up to bed because of the broken glass. Then I will come and give you a hand Florrie. But don't put any lights on just in case your blinds are down.' He nearly said 'too', but managed to catch himself in time.

'Thank you Alan. You are a dear,' Florrie said, and walked round to her place carrying Michael.

When Jean and Alan entered her cottage there was the noise of crunching glass beneath their feet. They took the boys straight upstairs and Jean tucked them up and kissed them both. Both boys had droopy eyes so it wouldn't take them long to get back to sleep.

Alan stopped Jean on the stairs and he gave her a very deep kiss. 'I am so glad you are all right, Mrs Drummond. I was very worried about you,' he said, very tongue-in-cheek.

'I felt very guilty lying to Florrie, and I can't disguise it because I blush so easily. Thank God it was dark so she couldn't see it,' she whispered.

'It always seems worse when people have your colouring. That beautiful skin and that lovely auburn hair. If I am not careful I'll take you on the stairs right here and now,' said Alan reaching for her.

'Don't you dare! The boys aren't even asleep yet.'

'I'll bet they are. Anyway I had better go and see if Florrie is all right as promised. I'll be back later.'

'By the way, what is the time?'

Squinting at his watch at the bottom of the stairs he said, 'Ten o'clock.'

'Is that all? I thought it was a lot later. I didn't get to finish my drink at the City Arms.'

'Must go and see to Florrie. See you when I've finished there.' He was out the front door in a flash.

Jean went to the cupboard under the stairs and took a broom and dustpan and brush. She started to sweep some of the glass up as best she could when a shadow blocked out what little of the moonlight there was. Her hand went to her throat and she jumped nearly out of her skin.

She relaxed when the shadow spoke. It was Mr Barstow the butcher from down the bridge. 'I am sorry. I didn't mean to startle you. I came to see if you and the boys are safe.'

'Yes thank you, Mr Barstow. I have lost both upstairs and downstairs windows but Alan Armstrong is coming back to give me hand with the blinds when he has finished at Mrs Hunter's.'

'That's very kind of him. He's a good lad. I never seem to see you down the shelter, Mrs Drummond,' Mr Barstow said reproachfully.

'That's right. You see, I can't stand closed in places. But I always take the boys down there and Florrie, Mrs Hunter, bless her heart, always keeps an eye on them,' said Jean.

Just then Alan walked in. 'Is that you Mr Barstow?'

'Oh, hello Alan. Mrs Drummond said you'd be coming back to help her with the blackout blinds. If I was a bit younger I'd lend a hand, but with my arthritis I can't reach over my head. I am sorry lad.'

'That's okay Mr Barstow. I am sure Mrs Drummond and I can manage between us.'

'I'd better let you young 'uns get on with it then.'

'Thank you so much for offering to help Mr Barstow. It was very kind of you,' said Jean.

'Goodnight Alan. Goodnight Mrs Drummond. Give my regards to Mr Drummond when you next write.'

'Oh I will. Goodnight, and thanks.'

'Goodnight,' said Alan.

'That was very nice of him,' said Jean, 'although he frightened the life out of me when I was sweeping up some of the glass.'

Alan had brought his torch with him so they were able to see a bit better. He swept up most of the glass whilst Jean held the torch and between them they managed to fix the blackout curtain back.

Alan went outside and tapped on the window frame as a signal to Jean to switch on the light. He tapped twice on the frame and Jean switched it off.

He walked in the door and switched the light back on. 'That seems to work okay. No chinks of light are showing. I'll come back tomorrow to measure up for new panes of glass, and fix the upstairs blind then as well.'

'How was Florrie's home?'

'She was very lucky. There was no damage. All these cottages along the Portsmouth Road side seem to have caught the full brunt of the explosions.'

'Do you want a cup of tea, Alan?'

'No thank you. I just want you again,' he said, pulling her into his arms.

Jean managed to sidestep him and say, 'No, Alan. It mustn't happen again. Ever.'

'Ever! You can't mean that, Jean.'

'Please don't make it any harder for me. Please. Florrie walks in any time when she thinks I'm on my own so she could easily catch us in the act.'

'What if I come just when there's an air raid?' Alan pleaded.

'I shouldn't have let you earlier. It must have been my fear as I was very vulnerable then. So please don't ask me. I

am a fairly weak person with the will-power of a split pea.'
Despite himself he could not help smiling at that, and Jean
continued, 'And it's not fair to Tom or me.'

'All right, Jean. I promise not to put temptation in your
way.'

'Thank you Alan. Now about that cup of tea.'

'No I don't think I'll have one thanks. I had better go in
case my feelings get the better of me. So I will come by
tomorrow at lunchtime to measure up for the glass.'

Before Jean could answer Alan she heard Florrie calling,
'Cooee. Coooeee.'

Jean gave Alan a look as if to say, 'I told you so.'

'We're in the front Florrie. Alan was just going. I was
trying to persuade him to stay for a cup of tea but he said
no.'

'Yes,' said Alan. 'I had better get back to HQ to see if
there is anything more I can do down there.'

'Thank you for all your help Alan. I'll see you tomorrow
lunchtime then. Goodnight.'

'Goodnight Florrie, Jean. Till tomorrow then.'

'Goodnight Alan,' said Florrie.

'Phew! What an evening. Would you stay for a cup of tea
Florrie?'

'Yes I would like that. Please.'

Florrie got the teacups out while Jean put the kettle on
and went to the cupboard and reached in for the biscuit
barrel. 'I hope there's some in here... We're in luck. There
are a couple of custard creams, half a dozen digestive, great
for dipping in the tea, and chocolate bourbons. I don't
know how old they are. Do you want to risk it?'

'Yes, why not.'

The kettle was just about to boil, and Jean got up to see
to the tea.

Out of the blue Florrie said, 'Did Alan go to the HQ
tonight Jean?'

Jean had her back to Florrie, which was just as well as she was blushing again, and trying to act normally she answered, 'I suppose so. Why?' She took her time making the tea, warming the pot with hot water, swilling it round, and then pouring the water out and putting the tea in it. Her blush was easing off so she turned around.

Florrie was watching her closely when she answered, 'Well, he must have flown to the bridge to get there before the first explosion.'

'Yes. I suppose he must. But I was too busy being scared to death to worry about him.'

'Mmm. Will you be coming down to the shelter now you've had a scare, or not?' asked Florrie.

Jean's reactions to Florrie's earlier question had eased off completely, so she could answer normally, 'I definitely won't be going back to the shelter. But I'll admit that I came close to it earlier though.'

They drank their tea in silence until Jean said, 'It's bad enough just taking the boys down there. God knows what I'll do when this one arrives.' She rubbed her stomach. 'I suppose I will owe it to the poor little mite to take it down there. But in the words of Miss Scarlett, "After all, tomorrow is another day",' she said, in a passable Southern States accent.

They were both laughing and on that happy note Florrie said goodnight and that she would see Jean tomorrow to help her clear up the mess.

Chapter Seven

In the light of day you could see the extent of the damage. They said it was the bomb that dropped on one of the water beds that caused all the damage to Thames Cottages.

There were small pieces of metal embedded in the wall of Jean's cottage. I was damn lucky, thought Jean, surveying the damage. Florrie came through from the back and said, 'You were very lucky not to have any more damage than you have. I've just come back from the bridge and there is talk of an unexploded bomb on the Rec. The police are keeping everyone away.'

'Has anyone been hurt?'

'I didn't hear that anyone had, although old Mrs Strudwick fell out of bed when the siren went off and broke her leg,' Florrie said, grinning.

'Well I had better start clearing up. Were the boys all right when you came through the back yard, Florrie?'

'Yes, they were playing quietly.'

'That's what worries me. When they are playing quietly they are always up to something.'

'You worry too much Jean.'

'I know. I'm a born worrier.' At that moment Jeff came through from the back brandishing a large chunk of metal.

'What is this Mummy? Is it a bomb?'

Jean went deathly pale as she took the piece of metal from Jeff's hand. 'It is a little bit of a bomb dear,' playing down the significance of it. Jeff ran off with his prize and calling to Michael. She looked at Florrie who was watching her with a frightened expression.

'I'll say this. You were damn lucky.'

'That could have hit me when I came through the door. I don't know what to say. Just the thought of it makes me shudder.' At that moment her baby chose to start kicking. 'Ooh! Ooh!' she cried, clutching her stomach, 'the baby's kicking.'

'Come and sit down. It must have been all the excitement of last night. Come on,' Florrie urged, 'and I'll make us a nice cup of Rosie Lee.'

Jean smiled despite herself. 'Why is it that folk think that drinking tea is "the be-all and end-all" cure for everything that ails us?'

'Well tea didn't end all for you, did it? And the gin isn't any good either – is it?'

This time Jean really laughed. 'What would I do without you Florrie Hunter?' hugging Florrie to her bosom.

'I don't know. Muddle through somehow I expect,' Florrie suggested.

'Tell me something Jean. Did Alan go straight down to the bridge last night? He must really have flown there to avoid that first bomb.'

Jean stared at Florrie and was going to lie to her. She thought better of it and told her the truth, or at least most of it.

'He didn't make it to the HQ as the first explosion came when I was opening the front door. He pushed me in, and when there was the big flash of light he pushed me into the Morrison shelter and came in after me. Of course you wouldn't have seen the flash.'

'And?'

'And what?' asked Jean.

'And did he stay here all that time?'

Jean looked away and took her time answering. She took a deep breath as if making up her mind and turned back to Florrie. 'Yes, he was here all the time.'

'I thought so.'

'How did you know?'

'Well to tell the truth, I guessed as much last night. I knew Alan couldn't have got to the HQ and that he must have stayed here. I didn't know it was all the time though.'

All Jean could say was, 'Oh.'

'Don't worry, your secret is safe with me.'

'I know that Florrie, but... but...' Jean had started crying softly.

'Jean don't cry. Did he hurt you?'

'Oh no Florrie. It was so wonderful, and Alan was so gentle.'

'I should hope so. But next time don't leave your knickers on the bed for all to see.'

'Oh!' said Jean mortified. 'There won't be a next time and I told Alan that.'

'Well wipe your eyes and drink your tea. What did he say when you told him that?'

'He told me he loved me and said he always had. And that's as far as we got before you walked in last night.'

'Does he know that you are pregnant?'

'No. I haven't told him yet. It will be pretty obvious soon. We weren't exactly talking while he was here. Actually it came as a bit of a surprise when the all-clear sounded, as we must have dropped off to sleep. You should have seen us move in the dark. In my panic I couldn't find my panties when I got dressed.'

'Hello, is anyone there?' Alan called from the front door.

'Yes, we're through here. Come and have that cup of tea you declined last night,' said Florrie.

'No,' Jean whispered.

'You've got to face him some time,' whispered Florrie.

'But not now...'

Before any more could be said, Alan was pushing the door open to the kitchen.

'Morning, ladies! And how are we this morning,?'

'Fine thanks,' said Jean and Florrie together.

'You were very lucky that there wasn't more damage, Jean.'

'Yes I know. Florrie was telling me that. Jeffery came in a little while ago with a huge piece of shrapnel,' said Jean.

'What really happened last night?' asked Florrie. Both Jean and Alan turned guiltily towards Florrie. Florrie, seeing their expressions, burst out laughing. 'I mean with the raid. There wasn't much warning before the bombs started failing.'

'Oh... oh.' Alan answered Florrie as understanding dawned on him. 'Apparently it was a couple of bombers on their way back home that hadn't dropped all their bombs.'

'So they decided to drop them on us?' Jean asked and looked up from pouring the tea.

'Exactly,' said Alan.

'Here's your tea, Alan,' Jean said pushing a cup and saucer toward him. Their hands accidentally touched and Jean snatched her hand away as though she'd had an electric shock.

Florrie noticed her friend's reaction and smiled wryly, all the time thinking that Jean was going to have a hard time pretending nothing had happened to her and Alan.

Alan sat sipping his tea and all was quiet until Florrie spoke. 'Well this won't do. I had better go and clear up the back yard in case there's some more shrapnel around.'

'Do you have to go?' Jean asked, hoping she would not leave her alone with Alan.

'Yes, I am afraid so. Anyway I am sure Alan won't bite you,' Florrie said as she walked off laughing.

'I had better get on and do the measuring up for the glass. Is it all right if I go upstairs, Jean?'

'Of course it is. I have to clear these cups away and put the boiler on for some washing. Do you know the way Alan?' But he had already gone up the stairs.

Alone with her thoughts Jean got on with the clearing up of the tea things and filling up the gas copper for the washing.

Eventually Alan came downstairs and into the kitchen where Jean was sorting the washing out into separate piles. As she walked past the kitchen window she was in full sunshine and silhouette, and the sunlight made her hair glow as if it was on fire. He ran his eyes over her body that he had got to know so well last night. His eyes went back to her waistline. The shock that was in his voice caused Jean to turn around in alarm.

'Oh God. No!'

'What's wrong? Tell me please. You look as though you have seen a ghost.' Then Jean followed his eyes and saw that he was looking at her stomach. She hastily grabbed a towel to cover herself and her embarrassment.

'Why didn't you tell me you were pregnant, Jean?'

'You haven't given me much of a chance to tell you anything, have you? We haven't really been alone since last night. I was going to tell you later.' She was angry at the reproach in his voice as though it was a sin to be pregnant.

'I wouldn't have touched you if I had known,' he said looking hurt.

'Alan Armstrong get out of my house,' said Jean angrily. 'Where do you get off acting like God? Would you have touched me if I didn't have Tom's baby inside me?' She was more angry than she had ever been in her life. And hurt. And with the anger came the tears. 'Just get out Alan.' She turned away from him.

Alan pulled Jean toward him and was shaking her to

make her calm down and saying to her, 'Jean, Jean. Calm down before you hurt yourself. You misunderstood me, Jean. I didn't mean it to sound like that. I love you Jean. And I wouldn't hurt you for the world. I just meant I wouldn't have touched you in a sexual way, because I might have hurt the baby.' Alan wiped her tears away with his handkerchief and kissed her on the forehead. 'Can we still be just good friends?'

'Oh yes, Alan. I'm so sorry I lost my temper,' she said looking up at him. The longing in his eyes was quite painful to witness.

He shook himself and said, 'Try not to get too angry with me, or in my presence. You're very beautiful when you're angry and I might not be able to help myself.'

Jean could laugh now and she felt totally at ease again with him.

'I should go and buy that glass otherwise I'll be fitting it in darkness. See you later Jean.'

With that he shut the front door gently behind him. He had come as a hopeful lover and left as a very good friend.

Chapter Eight

The war carried on around Jean and Florrie. They had watched with the children as a fleet of small boats went up the Thames toward London. They wondered where they were going, but at the time one didn't ask too many questions. One accepted.

They were sitting on the opposite side of the river from where they lived. Florrie's cottage was visible from where they were sitting and Jean was saying how nice the roses looked that grew up around her arched doorway.

It was in the middle of one of their picnics that the boats started coming up the river. Large ocean-going ships; medium sized boats that would sleep two or possibly three people; and tiny ones, no more than rowing boats, which looked as though they would not reach the next bend, let alone their destination.

Jeff, Michael and Ken watched in fascination as the boats kept coming, their biscuits and lemonade forgotten their mouths open at the spectacle of so many craft. The boys waved to the men on the boats and sometimes the men waved back. Even Jean and Florrie waved if they saw a particularly nice-looking chap sail past.

It was not until a couple of days later that Florrie rushed over to Jean's shouting with excitement, 'Jean! Jean! Did you hear the news on the radio?' Jean shook her head. Florrie continued hardly pausing for breath and said, 'You know all those boats we saw the other day? They were all going to Dunkirk.'

'Where's Dunkirk?' asked Jean, but before Florrie could answer Jeff piped up and said, 'Were they all going on a picnic too, Mummy?'

Both Jean and Florrie laughed but Jean said, 'I don't think so darling. Perhaps they were joining the Navy.'

'That was exactly what they were doing, joining the Royal Navy.'

'What on earth do you mean?'

'Exactly that. They were going to join the Navy across in France on a big rescue mission. Apparently most of the British Expeditionary Forces are trapped on the beaches there with the Germans snapping at their heels, and being strafed by the Luftwaffe. They have gone to help get them off and bring them home.'

'What! Some of those boats didn't look as though they'd get to London, let alone across the Channel to Dunkirk.'

'I know. That is exactly what they did though. The Prime Minister is so proud of the effort that was involved. He said that without them thousands of soldiers would have been taken prisoner or killed.'

'So we witnessed history in the making. Well I never.'

*

'Jean, Jeeean. Where are you?' Florrie clicked her fingers in front of Jean's face.

'Oh, I am sorry. I was miles away. I was just thinking about Tom and wondering where he was shipped off to.'

'It must be a worry for you. I am just glad that Joe's in Scotland, although I don't suppose they are safe anywhere, even in Scotland.'

'No. And now that Germany has invaded Norway they can fly their planes straight across the North Sea to Scotland.'

'Oh. Thanks for that bit of comfort. That is all I needed to make my day,' laughed Florrie.

'I'm sorry, I didn't think before speaking,' apologised Jean.

Tom had come home on embarkation leave early in October. He just breezed in one Friday morning and said that he had until Monday morning before reporting back.

Jean was sweeping the back yard and Tom had frightened the life out of her when he came up behind her and put his arms about her.

'Tom! Whatever are you doing here this time of day?'

'That's charming! No "it's lovely to see you", and no kiss of welcome. Come here and give me a kiss,' Tom demanded.

Jean complied and said to come indoors and she would put the kettle on.

'You are beautiful you know Jean! Don't bother with the tea. Let's go to bed.'

'I can't as Ken is only over at Florrie's and he will be over soon.'

'If that's all that's worrying you then there is no worry.' Tom popped over to Florrie's and was back in a tick. 'Now come upstairs.'

Jean followed Tom up and he pushed her gently onto the bed and started to undress her. He was kissing her gently and being very careful of her stomach. She was due in a few weeks time.

'What did you say to Florrie?' asked Jean.

'Just if she would mind watching Ken for a while. Now come here,' he said to Jean, gently pulling her toward him. He proceeded, ever so tenderly, to make love to her.

She was so surprised at his tenderness that it was about the only time in the past few years that she had really enjoyed sex with him. It was a pity he couldn't have been like this all the other times when it seemed that he only satisfied himself, and left her high and dry. This time he was very mindful of her condition, which was probably why he was very loving and patient with her.

★

'Come down off that cloud you're on and tell me what happened when Tom saw Alan in the pub?'

'Well nothing actually. I was on tenterhooks in case Alan came in and he was bound to, it being Friday,' said Jean. 'Fortunately Joe and Tom were talking to each other, so they didn't see the expression on Alan's face when he walked in. It was like... like... like the whole world had collapsed around him. He looked at me with such hurt in his eyes, as if it was all my fault that Tom was sitting beside me, and it nearly broke my heart to see him so hurt.'

'I thought that that was all over between you and him.'

'It is over. The sex bit, but he is still in love with me.' Jean put both hands over her heart very dramatically fluttering her eyelashes. 'He said as much the other day when I bumped into him.' They both smiled, Jean a little wistfully.

'Anyway, what happened when he spoke to Tom? It was a pity I was stuck in the loo talking to Mrs Green.'

'He said, "Hello Tom. Hello Joe. Nice to see you both home together." Very restrained, I thought, but Tom didn't know anything so he wouldn't have been suspicious. Anyway, I thought it best not to tell Tom about it. What could I say to him anyway? "Dear, I made love with Alan Armstrong in the Morrison shelter, and it was great." No, I couldn't have done that to him; I still love him and I wouldn't hurt him for the world. Specially now.'

'No,' said Florrie, 'what an anticlimax.'

'Alan recovered quite quickly but you should have seen the look he gave me. When Tom saw him he asked Alan to sit down and have a drink. That was when you came back from the loo Florrie, so you know the rest.'

'He didn't stay long, did he? He just collected the Club money, drank his drink and left. Presumably he went back into the other bar,' Jean sighed.

'How about taking the boys up the Rec to play on the swings?' said Florrie, to relieve the tension and change the subject.

'Okay,' said Jean, 'but I'll have to run upstairs for a cardigan. I won't be a tick.'

Florrie went out the back to call the boys to tell them they are going up the Rec.

'Are we going to have a picnic, Mum?' asked Michael hopefully.

'No, you are not. In any case, your life is one long picnic. Perhaps tomorrow.'

'Oh goody! Jeff we are going on a picnic tomorrow.'

'Oh goody!' echoed Jeff.

'Now wait a minute. I only said we might,' Florrie said in exasperation.

'I'm ready. Let's go,' Jean said.

Florrie and Jean held the boys' hands when they crossed the Portsmouth Road. It was far too busy to let them cross on their own. Once over the other side they let go of them. They promptly ran off toward the Rec. As usual Kenny toddled behind quite happily. He was two now and quite sturdy, and Jeff was four. Where did the time go?

As they walked down Windmill Lane their eyes were drawn to the water bed that the bomb had dropped on. Fortunately the Water Board had not got around to filling it with water before the bomb struck, so it didn't disrupt anything.

Michael and Jeff were nearly at the Rec and were racing to see the crater where the other bomb had dropped.

Florrie said, 'Are you thinking about that night, Jean?'

'Yes, I think I always will, at least as long as there is a waterworks here. Thank heavens there hasn't been a night like that again.'

'Do you mean the night of passion?' laughed Florrie.

'No, of course not. Though that was rather nice.'

'Jean!'

Jean laughed. 'I meant the bombing. I was scared stiff whilst that was going on. It's a wonder I didn't have this baby that night, what with one thing and another.'

What Jean had said to Florrie was true. The night of passion with Alan had been rather nice. In fact she could not describe how nice it had been. Tom did not seem to think of Jean's needs, just satisfying himself. But despite that she still loved Tom.

'When is it due? It can't be far off now.'

'In a couple of weeks' time. Early November.'

'Ooh.' A sound of disappointment came from the boys. 'The hole's gone. That's not fair.'

'Now don't be silly. How can you and Jeff play football with a huge great hole in the middle of the pitch, eh?' Florrie asked Michael. 'In any case, leaving it like that was dangerous. Now go and play on the swings.'

They went and played on the swings as good as gold, taking it in turns to push Ken on the swings.

There were two little girls there and when Jeff and Michael saw them they started showing off by pushing Ken higher and higher. Typical boys. Florrie had to step in as Ken was becoming frightened.

No more was said about 'that night', and the two friends sat in companionable silence.

They sat there for a while, each with her own thoughts, speaking only occasionally, until it was time to go home.

Chapter Nine

Jean and Florrie were going to take the boys to the cinema for a treat. *Snow White and the Seven Dwarfs* was playing down at Esher but Jean did not feel too good so the boys were playing in Jean's front room instead, with the small Hornby 00 gauge train set Tom had bought Jeff and Ken when he was home on embarkation leave. It was fairly new and still a novelty to them.

Today was the first time Michael had seen it and he thought it was great. Jean was pleased for the boys that Tom had bought it, but they could ill afford it as they really needed other things. She did not argue with him as she had wanted his last leave to be special, for she did not know when she would see him again.

While the boys were playing with the train set, Florrie was helping Jean sort out some baby clothes.

'It's just as well you don't believe in having pink or blue for your baby clothes, or Ken's wouldn't be any good if it's is a girl,' observed Florrie.

'That is why I only knitted white or pale yellow.'

'Ooh. Is this new? I haven't seen it before. It's gorgeous,' said Florrie holding up a beautifully smocked tiny silk dress.

'Yes. I have been making it while you've been down the shelter with the boys. I did it to take my mind off the fact that there was an air raid on.'

'Where did you get the material for it?'

'It was my wedding dress. I definitely won't be wearing it again, so thought I'd make a few things out of it.'

'Well, I must say you've done a smashing job of it,' said Florrie admiringly.

'I am going to make myself a couple of blouses out of it. And I was going to make you one too.'

'Oh no. You can't do that.'

'Why not? You deserve it. So I won't take no for an answer. So there,' Jean added with a smile.

'Thank you Jean.' Florrie gave Jean a hug.

'By the way Jean, did anything come of that business with Lil down the pub?'

'Yes. She popped round a couple of days later to ask if I could do some of her dresses for her. She said she would pay me five bob a dress, but I said that two and six would be enough. She insisted on five bob, so five bob it is.'

'She can well afford it. You have seen for yourself the amount of trade they do. Good for you! I am so glad something came of it.'

They were quiet for a moment sorting out and folding some more baby things when Jean said, 'Alan called round the other night.'

'What did he want?'

'Nothing.'

'He must have wanted something,' Florrie said, and added, 'didn't he say anything?'

'Yes he did. He said that he still loves me and wants to come round of an evening. I said that that wasn't fair. Then he asked me if I didn't feel anything for him. Well, what could I say? That I love him too and that I also love Tom. I didn't tell him that, but I wanted to. Oh how I wanted to! Instead I told him that he should forget me and find himself a single girl to love, someone who could love him unconditionally. I daren't tell him I love him, I wanted to but just didn't. That wouldn't be fair to him – he would expect more than I can give him. It's as much my fault as his so I can't blame him.' Jean took a deep breath and sighed.

'You haven't encouraged him have you? What did he say when you said, "Find another girl"?'

'He had that hurt little boy's look that is so endearing. God, I want him so. But he will never know how much.'

Florrie had put the kettle on and was making the inevitable pot of tea: the cure for everything.

Just then, Jean's waters broke without warning. 'Oh my God, my waters have broken! What am I to do?' But Florrie took charge. She rushed upstairs to get a towel and a blanket for Jean to wrap around herself and said, 'Don't move. I'm going down the pub.'

'This is no time to go and have a drink,' laughed Jean between bouts of pain.

'Don't be daft. I am going to ring for an ambulance from there. Stay quiet,' ordered Florrie.

She grabbed her coat and dashed to the pub. When she got there all breathless Lil asked her what was wrong and Florrie told her and asked if she could use the phone. Lil said she'd do the phoning and told Florrie to get back to Jean.

Alan heard all this and went round to Jean's on the double. When he got there Jean was obviously surprised to see him and was about to berate him when he forestalled her and said, 'I heard Florrie in the pub and I thought I could stay here with the boys while Florrie goes to the hospital with you.'

Just then Florrie got back saying the ambulance is on its way and what was Alan doing there – hardly without a pause for breath. But Jean put her hand out to Florrie and something in Jean's expression stopped her from continuing. Jean managed to say that Alan was staying with the boys.

By this time the boys were standing in the doorway wide-eyed and frightened at the goings-on. It was Alan who put their fears to rest by saying, 'Hey, how would you boys like it if I put you all to bed?'

Michael piped up. 'Me too?' he asked hopefully. Alan looked across at Florrie who was holding Jean's hand. Florrie smiled at Michael and nodded. He was jumping up and down with glee and saying, 'Jeff, Jeff, I can stay the night with you.' Jeff was obviously pleased and although Ken did not know what was going on he was smiling and jumped up and down too.

Alan told the boys to get upstairs and put their pyjamas on, at which Florrie said she would go and get Michael a pair. Jean told her he could wear a pair of Jeff's and told Alan where to find them.

At that instant the ambulance arrived, bells ringing. Florrie helped Jean to her feet and then the ambulance men took over.

Chapter Ten

Jean gave birth without too much trouble to a little girl of eight pounds three ounces at quarter past two in the morning.

Florrie had been pacing up and down with frustration as they would not let her in the delivery room. Now she knew why in the films the expectant fathers were always depicted as marching up and down.

At last the doctor came out to see her and told her the weight of the baby and that it was a girl, and that Jean was all right, though she was sleeping. He asked the nurse to get Florrie a cup of tea but she declined and asked if she could sit in with her friend instead. The doctor said that she could for a while.

Florrie crept in and saw that Jean was indeed sleeping. That girl can sleep though practically anything, she thought, smiling as she sat down.

Jean looked perfectly all right and she definitely did not look as though she had been through nearly six hours of labour. Eventually she stirred and saw Florrie sitting there, and smiled. Florrie smiled back but Jean was already asleep.

At five thirty in the morning Jean woke up fully and found Florrie sleeping with her head in her arms, resting on the side of bed. She shook her gently and Florrie sat up with reluctance, wiping the sleep from her eyes, stretching and yawning.

'Good morning dear. How are you feeling?'

'Fine, thank you. Have you seen the baby yet?' asked Jean.

'Not yet. All I know is that it is a little girl and that she weighs eight pounds three ounces.'

'I don't remember much about it as I was doped up to the eyeballs. I didn't hardly know what was going on. All that I can remember was the doctor saying, 'Push. Push. Stop pushing. Now one more push.' Then it was all over. The nurse took the baby and someone cleaned me up, and then I fell asleep.'

'The nurse should be bringing the baby in for a feed soon,' said Florrie. 'I'll wait until I have seen her then I had better get home so that Alan can get off home too.'

'Oh heavens, yes! I had forgotten about him.'

The nurse brought the baby wrapped in a hospital blanket and Florrie asked if she could hold it and have a look at it. The nurse said yes and handed the baby over to Florrie.

Peeping at the baby under the blanket she said, 'Oh Jean! She is beautiful and she has downy white blonde hair and big blue eyes. Here, have a look. She is smiling at me too,' said Florrie in wonder.

'It is probably wind,' said Jean laughing and holding out her arms for her baby.

'That's charming!' said Florrie, laughing too, and handing the baby back very gently to Jean.

'What are you going to call her?'

'I don't know yet. When I talked it over with Tom he said he didn't mind what I called it as long as it wasn't too long a name. So I'm still thinking about it.'

'Mrs Drummond,' interrupted the nurse, 'it's time to feed the baby.'

'I'd better be going to see how the boys are behaving,' said Florrie, as she leant over the baby to give Jean a kiss on the cheek. 'I'll bring your bag of things that we forgot last night this afternoon. Bye for now,' she said, waving as she went out the door.

Florrie arrived home at seven thirty and went straight to Jean's house. Alan had the boys up, washed and dressed and was giving them some porridge he had found in the cupboard. He was putting a dab of margarine on top of some bread and he had a pot of home-made blackcurrant jam already on the table.

Looking up he saw Florrie in the doorway surveying the scene smiling at him.

'How's Jean, Florrie?'

'She's fine. She had a little girl at about two fifteen this morning. And she's gorgeous.'

'Here. Sit down and have a cup of tea, you look worn out.'

She sat down thankfully and said, 'You seem to be well organised – quite domesticated.'

'Yes, Jeff showed me where things were, didn't you Jeff? Don't forget I live on my own. I have learnt to look after myself.'

'Yes,' Jeff mumbled through a mouthful of bread and jam. 'Where is Mummy, Aunty Florrie?' Florrie explained as best she could so that he and Ken could understand. Whether she got through to them was difficult to tell. They were too enraptured with having Alan looking after them to have been worried.

'How did they all behave last night Alan?'

'No problem at all really. I read them a story and they went to sleep quite quickly after I'd finished reading to them. I came down here and had a cup of tea, then fell asleep in the armchair. When are you going to see Jean again?'

'This afternoon. I have to take her bag of things in. In the rush last night we forgot them. At the moment she is wearing a hospital gown and you know how glamorous they are. A bit draughty around the nether regions!' laughed Florrie.

'Too true. I felt very embarrassed when I was in Kingston hospital and only had one of those gowns to wear. I think the hospital staff take delight in giving you one a few sizes too small. I had to go to the toilet down the hall, *and* during visiting hours! Anyway, there I was trying to clutch the back of this gown together down the back, all the while trying to look nonchalant. It was hard. Why do they make them like that?' he asked, laughing. 'How are you getting up there this afternoon?'

'Probably by bike, why?'

'I've been meaning to go to the Armstrong Siddeley offices with some plans, and I can use the firm's car, so if you like I can give you a lift there. What do you say to that?'

'That'd be great, but won't you get into trouble for doing that?' queried Florrie, obviously worried about it.

'No. Old Mr Greer, the owner, often wants me to go and get things for him so I often deviate from the route. Anyway the hospital is not much further. And I will spread the time out at the office, and come and pick you up about four, if that's all right with you?'

'It is, but are you sure you won't get into any trouble? I can easily go by bike?'

'Look, don't worry your pretty little head about it. Oh Lord,' he exclaimed as he caught sight of the mantel clock. 'I have to run. I'll pick you up at quarter to two.' With that he was gone; Florrie had not even thanked him properly.

★

As usual Florrie arranged for Mrs Mitchell to watch the boys. What would Jean and herself do without her to babysit for them? There was no doubt about it, she was a godsend.

When Alan picked her up he had a huge bunch of flowers in the back of the old Austin Seven.

'Ooh. What a lovely bunch of flowers. They are really beautiful.'

'I picked them from my mother's garden. She arranged them into that bunch. She used to be a professional florist. Would you mind taking them in for Jean please, Florrie?'

'No. Not at all. Jean will be delighted with them.'

And she was, only she blushed when Florrie told her who they were from.

Chapter Eleven

Jean came out of hospital and settled back down to a busy life of looking after the children and altering dresses. Apart from Lil, the landlady of the City Arms, she had quite a growing clientele, but there was only so much she could do with the spare time available to her. And since having this last baby she did not find much spare time at all.

Alan came round to see her and to ask how she was. She thanked him for the flowers and for looking after the boys in the evenings whilst Florrie was up at the hospital visiting her, giving Mrs Mitchell a rest.

'I enjoyed it, Jean. And I think the boys like me being here.'

'Oh, they did Alan. They haven't stopped talking about it.'

She had written to Tom and told him about the baby, and that she had decided to call her Janet.

It was now January '41 and she had not heard from Tom since October when he'd been home on embarkation leave. Needless to say she was beginning to worry. He'd never been much of a letter writer, but she usually received a letter from him on average once a month. She had taken into account that he was overseas, and that the mail was a bit erratic in wartime, but four months!

The worry was beginning to show in her attitude towards everything. Even the boys noticed something was wrong. It was not anything she did or said, it was a lack of doing. She was vague and absent-minded, and that's what Florrie noticed more than anything else. If it had not been for her, poor little Janet would not have been fed unless Jean was reminded. Florrie often caught Jean gazing into space.

Florrie bumped in to Alan down on Winter's Bridge one day and he asked her what was wrong with Jean. She had totally ignored him, and walked right past him. She had the baby with her propped up in her pram playing with the dangling toys that were suspended from the canopy of the pram, and he seemed to get more attention from the baby. In fact, he was quite hurt when Jean completely ignored him and carried on walking.

'She's worried about Tom. She hasn't heard from him since he went away.'

'That's nearly four months ago; not even a letter or a postcard?'

'No. Nothing. Even I am beginning to worry. Tom has never been much of a letter writer, but he has usually got in touch with her at least every few weeks. Joe will be home this weekend; he might be able help her. Suggest who to write to, that sort of thing. I am afraid that I can't seem to be able to get her out of this self-induced bout of vagueness. She's more and more like a zombie. It can't be post-natal depression, she was perfectly okay until just after Christmas.'

Alan had listened patiently whilst Florrie was telling her this, feeling concern for her but mostly concern for Jean. Things must be bad for Florrie to be so worried for Jean.

'Is there anything I can do for her?' Alan asked hopefully.

'I don't think so. I don't know what to do for her myself. I'll wait for the weekend for Joe to come home and see what he says.'

'I'll pop around to see her tomorrow lunchtime,' Alan told Florrie, 'and try and cheer her up.'

'Okay Alan. I'll probably see you then.'

★

When Alan arrived at Jean's the next day, everything was deathly quiet. He knocked on the door, but there was no answer. He was about to knock again when Florrie answered the door in tears. She held the door open for him. He rushed past her to find Jean sitting in the kitchen gazing into space, dry-eyed. In her hand she held a buff-coloured telegram. Alan took it gently from her hand, then read it.

It was a standard telegram from the War Office.

THE WAR OFFICE REGRETS TO INFORM YOU THAT BOMBARDIER THOMAS ALBERT DRUMMOND OF THE ROYAL ARTILLERY IS MISSING, PRESUMED KILLED IN ACTION.

Alan looked up at Florrie with raised eyebrows as if to say 'has she said anything?' She shook her head.

Since the telegram had arrived she had hardly moved a muscle, nor had she cried, nor spoken. Nothing. She just gazed into space.

Florrie had taken the boys next door to Mrs Beecham, and her daughter, Betty, was keeping an eye on them. The baby was in the front room gurgling away in the Morrison shelter.

'I don't know what to do for the best,' murmured Florrie.

'Hadn't you better get her doctor to come and see her?'

'Yes, that is a good idea. I'll nip to the pub and ask Lil if I can use her phone. Will you stay here while I go?' Alan nodded.

As Florrie left, she accidentally let the front door bang. With that Jean seemed to become aware of what was going on around her. She looked at Alan kneeling on the floor in front of her and at the telegram in his hands. And it was just like an awakening as she realised what had happened.

The floodgates just burst open and Jean started to cry. Softly at first and more loudly. Alan pulled her into his arms trying to comfort her, but really not sure what to do. He shushed her and stroked her hair and said that the telegram could be wrong. Tom was just missing. Not necessarily killed, just missing.

Jean had quietened down a bit by the time Florrie came back from phoning, but the tears were streaming down her face. 'The doctor will be here as soon as he can. Something has registered at last,' Florrie said, noticing Jean in Alan's arms.

'Yes. It was the bang of the door when you left that seemed to trigger something off. Did you actually speak to the doctor and tell him what had happened?' he asked.

'Yes, he had a patient with him. But he won't be too long.' At least I hope not, Florrie thought to herself.

Jean looked at Alan and said, 'It's all my fault that he is dead.'

'No it isn't.'

'If I hadn't have been here with you that night of the air raid he would still be alive.'

'He may still be alive,' said Alan shaking her gently. 'It is not your fault, and Tom was still in the country then. So how could it be your fault? You're just feeling guilty about it, so do I, but we didn't kill Tom. Do you hear me?' he asked, shaking her again. 'Do you hear me Jean? It is not our fault. It's this bloody war. That's what is to blame, this bloody war!'

'No. I am to blame, and you,' she cried. 'It's my fault, and yours!' She sucked her breath in through her teeth in short gasps and tugged at her hair. Alan pulled her towards him again in an effort to calm her. She pushed him away.

He was nearly in tears himself trying to convince her. Florrie was in tears. He did not find out if he had calmed her down, for at that moment Doctor Braithwaite walked through the open front door.

He took one look at Jean and said, 'She is in shock. If I give her an injection will you be able to look after the children, Mrs Hunter?'

'Yes, of course, Doctor. What about the baby though? She'll need a feed.'

'You will have to give her some powdered milk, it won't hurt for once. Now Alan, you help me get Mrs Drummond upstairs, and Mrs Hunter, you sit with her until she is asleep please. Good,' he said as Florrie nodded.

They helped Jean up the narrow staircase. The injection was already taking effect. Alan and the doctor laid her very gently on the bed. She was asleep when her head touched the pillow. Florrie took Jean's shoes off and put a blanket over her.

When they got back downstairs, the doctor told Florrie to keep things quiet for Jean, which she agreed to do. Then he left.

'I'd better be getting back to work or the boss will fire me. But I'll come round straight from work to see if she is all right, if that's okay, Florrie?'

'Of course it will be Alan. And thanks for all your help.'

'I am just sorry that I couldn't do much for her. See you later.' And with that he left and went back to work.

★

Jean slept until ten o'clock that night. She could not understand why it was so quiet, so she got up to investigate.

The boys were not in their room and the baby was not in the drawer that doubled as a cot. She went downstairs to see if they were there. They were not in the Morrison shelter either so she went into the kitchen.

Alan was asleep in the armchair snoring softly. But there was still no sign of the children. She shook Alan gently. He came to and was surprised to see her there. He was about to speak but she spoke first, and asked where the children were. They are over at Florrie's, he told her, and would be staying there all night.

'What are you doing here then?'

Hurt by her attitude, he said, 'I'll go if you would like me to.'

'I am sorry I was so sharp! I was just worried about the children.'

'They are fine. More to the point, how are you now? You gave us all quite a scare.'

'I am all right, but I still can't believe that Tom is dead. Sorry about earlier. It was—'

Alan interrupted her. 'You have nothing to apologise for.'

'What I was going to say was that it was wrong of me to blame you for that night. It was as much my fault as yours. In fact more my fault. And I realise that it isn't our fault he's dead. Please forgive me for saying such hurtful things to you.'

'Neither of us are to blame. It's what some people call fate. It was meant to be Jean. Probably because I love you so much, and wanted you.'

Jean put her fingers over his lips. 'Please don't talk like that, Alan. You know I won't leave Tom, especially now.' He turned her hand over and kissed her palm. It sent a thrill up her arm and she was about to protest when he pulled her into his arms and gave her a deep lingering kiss. She started to pull away but he was too strong for her so she just seemed to crumble in his arms. He lifted her up and carried her to the front room and laid her on the bed there. Very gently – so gently that she hardly felt it – he undressed her. Soon all she was wearing were her panties, brassiere and unbuttoned blouse.

It all seemed like a dream to Jean and she found couldn't raise a finger to stop him or help him. Then she realised that she did not want him to stop and wanted him as much as he wanted her. She felt so guilty but even then she did nothing to stop what was going to happen. In the end she pulled him to her and kissed him longingly, letting all her frustration out in that one kiss.

By this time Alan was fully undressed and had managed to get the rest of her clothes off without too much difficulty. The light was still on in the kitchen so there was plenty of light to see by.

He kissed her on the lips then moved down to her throat. His lips were everywhere; on her shoulders, and then on her breasts.

His hands were caressing her thighs and stomach. He could tell she was ready for him by her movements, she was writhing beneath him, but he wanted to carry on exploring her. He started to push his fingers into her but with a sudden swift movement and surprising strength she had managed to roll him over. She mounted him, lowering herself languorously onto him.

Alan was so surprised that he just lay there. Jean leant forward to kiss him, her breasts pushed against his chest. She stopped kissing him and her breasts hovered over him. He sucked her nipples, then he placed his hands on her hips and raised his own so that he was right inside her, as far as he could go. She groaned with desire and started to move up and down on him. She was in ecstasy, and started to move faster and faster. Alan was working with her, pushing his hips upwards. He was ready but he was holding back. He was waiting for her. She was saying, 'Alan, Alan. Oh Alan, I do love you.' Then she sank onto his chest shuddering with spent passion.

She stayed where she was for a while. His climax came at the same instant as hers for he could not hold back any longer. He held her close to his chest.

He managed to pull the blankets over them both and kissed her gently.

'I have never had such good sex, Jean. You were gorgeous,' he whispered in her ear.

From the light in the kitchen he could see her embarrassed blush, but she managed to speak. 'I always seem to be blushing and apologising to you.'

'That is what is so refreshing about you, your lack of, lack of...' He was at a loss for words.

'Morals,' she interrupted him.

He could not help laughing as he said, 'Of course not. What I meant was your lack of inhibitions. Yes, that is it. Lack of inhibitions.'

'Oh, that! What does that mean?'

'Come here and I'll show you.' And then Alan pushed her from the top of him and started to make love to her again.

Chapter Twelve

Jean still didn't know whether Tom was alive or dead. The Red Cross were doing all they could in trying to find him but were having no luck.

They had found his two brothers, Fred and Walter; they were captured in Crete, on the same day as Tom was reported missing. They were separated from each other now, but were not injured.

So Jean was in the same position as she was when she had first heard the news in January, and it was now July.

The pain had eased gradually over the months, but she would have liked to know what her position was. Either Tom was dead, or alive: which?

She had to wait. She knew that the Red Cross was doing all they could in trying to find Tom and others like him in his position, but what was so frustrating was that there was nothing she could do.

At least she was still getting Tom's allotment every week, and so had some money coming in apart from the money she got for doing the dress alterations.

Alan still came round very discreetly, usually during an air raid, unless he was on duty down at the ARP Headquarters at Winter's Bridge. He would come when an air raid was on at night; there was little chance of him being seen owing to the blackout precautions. It was a bit more risky during the day.

Mrs Mitchell saw him going into Jean's one day when there was a raid. She had been late going to the shelter as she had been locked in her outside toilet. A yard broom had fallen down when she had shut the door and somehow it had jammed it. It had fallen between the toilet door and the greenhouse. She had struggled to free herself and at last managed it.

When she saw him going into Jean's house she said hello to him and gave him a large wink. He had the grace to blush, and she chuckled and dashed down to the shelter.

He got into Jean's house and leant against the front door breathing deeply as if he was out of breath. She saw him and asked him what on earth was the matter. When he told her she said, 'Thank God it was Mrs Mitchell! Anyone else would have spread it around Long Ditton by now and would be pounding down the doors. She won't tell anyone.'

'That does it,' he said. 'I'll only come at night. It's safer then. It is unlikely anyone will see me coming in then. Your reputation will be safe.'

'Oh Alan. Come here,' she said smiling. 'You are a darling. Always thinking of my reputation. Thank you.' She kissed him and they got onto the bed in the Morrison shelter. They did not make love, just lay there talking and kissing until the all-clear went.

Jeff and Ken came back from the shelter with Florrie. They were full of laughter. Alan had gone back to the factory the minute the all-clear had sounded.

'What are you two laughing at?' asked Jean.

'Mummy, it was ever so funny. The "Thunder Box" had just been emptied, and...'

'Don't call it that. I don't know where you got that expression from in any case. Call it a toilet please.' She had spoken firmly to the boys, but inwardly she was smiling at the term they had used for the chemical toilet. The boys went out to the back yard looking disappointed that Jean would not let Jeff finish the story.

Florrie finished off the story after the three boys had gone out to the back yard. 'You know they empty the loo every week?' Not waiting for an answer, she continued, 'They had just emptied it. Anyway those two sisters that are as deaf as a post, you know the ones I mean?' asked Florrie of Jean.

'Oh yes, the ones that live over the Dairy.'

'Yes that's them. Well, anyway, they went to the toilet and switched the light on. You know yourself that has the effect of a magic lantern show throwing their silhouette on the curtain. No one puts the light on in there. But they did. Consequently there were these two deaf old dears going to the toilet chatting away not knowing they are being observed and heard by everyone. It was just like Niagara Falls, too!'

Jean laughed at that, but Florrie had not finished so she continued. 'What made things worse was that the boys started laughing. I tried to quieten them down but they had started the whole shelter off laughing. It was a shame really as the poor old dears didn't know what everyone was laughing at. They even asked when they came out from behind the curtain.' Both Jean and Florrie were killing themselves laughing. 'But that started everyone off laughing again. I'll kill those boys, the little beggars.' They continued to laugh. Jean took a breath between laughing to say, 'Oh dear,' but it started her off again.

When they had calmed down Jean put the kettle on for the inevitable cup of tea.

Florrie took a sip of tea and asked, 'Did Alan come round today?'

'Yes. Why do you ask?'

'I just wondered. He wasn't down the shelter. Someone commented on it. But some bright spark said that he was probably in the one over the Rec.'

'Apparently Mrs Mitchell saw him coming here. Just as well it was her, she won't say anything.'

'Please be careful Jean,' pleaded Florrie.

'He has decided not to come during the daytime raids, only when the night-time ones are on. That meeting with Mrs Mitchell put the wind up him. Anyone else and it could have meant trouble,' said Jean with a sigh.

Noticing the sigh Florrie asked Jean if she had heard anything from the War Office.

'Afraid not. It's the not knowing that is getting me down. If Tom was dead, God forbid, at least I could make the necessary changes to my life.'

'Like marrying Alan?'

'Yes I suppose so, but that's not what I meant; although he hasn't asked me in so many words, we seemed to have taken it for granted. I've told Alan that as long as there is a chance that Tom is alive I wouldn't leave him.' Jean was quiet for a moment then continued, 'It is funny really, but I love them both. Do you think that is possible Florrie?'

Florrie thought about the question for a while and said, 'Yes I think so. But you must love them in different ways, Jean.'

'Well of course I do, but it is difficult to explain in what way.'

'Try and tell me what the differences are.'

'Like I said, it is difficult but I'll try.' Jean paused to think a while, then said, 'Tom has a calming influence on me. He is steady and a good father to the boys and very generous to us. I would be quite happy to spend the rest of my life with him.' She poured them both another cup of tea to give herself time to gather her thoughts about Alan.

'Now Alan, he is the total opposite to Tom. Ready to take a risk. He makes me laugh,'

'Doesn't Tom make you laugh?'

'Oh yes. But Alan makes me laugh at myself and at silly little things. At the things we do and at life in general. He is so thoughtful,' and here Jean blushed and looked away from Florrie, 'especially in bed. God, I am like a nymphomaniac where he is concerned. It may sound stupid to you, but I can't wait for an evening air raid for him to get here.' At this Florrie raised her eyebrows, but Jean seeing this said, 'Oh no. Not for the sex bit, but because I like being with him. Although that aspect of it is good as well. Does that sound too awful, Florrie?'

'Of course not Jean.'

They were interrupted by a male voice calling Jean from the front door. 'Mrs Drummond, Mrs Drummond.'

'Who on earth...' She went to the front room and there was Mr Taylor from the factory with little Janet under his arm. 'Oh my God. How did you get out?' There she was, cooing away in Mr Taylor's arms as good as gold.

'Thank you Mr Taylor, I am so sorry. I don't understand it. One minute she was asleep on the bed there and the next...' Jean did not finish what she was about to say and her hands flew to her mouth in horror at what could have happened to the poor little soul. But Mr Taylor said. 'Don't you worry yourself over it. She came to no harm and you know she is well looked after when you put her out in the pram.'

That was very true. Many times she had got Janet ready to take her to the clinic and she had left her outside in her pram while she herself got ready. A couple of times when she came out she found that Janet was covered in chocolate and she had to go and change her again. It was the men from the Perspex factory who were having a break at Mrs Raymond's who spoiled her. Mrs Raymond's was the cottage next to hers that had been converted to a little general store and café.

'Yes I know that Mr Taylor, but I can't understand how she actually got out there. And the thought of what could have happened, especially with the Portsmouth Road right outside... It doesn't bear thinking about.'

'No harm done. She was just sitting in your front porch playing with this piece of a toy car. The gate was shut, fortunately.'

'But I still can't believe it, she isn't even crawling yet.'

Mr Taylor still had hold of Janet who held her arms out to Jean.

'Thank you so much for bringing her in Mr Taylor. It is very kind of you,' Jean thanked him.

'Goodbye ladies.'

'Goodbye,' said both Jean and Florrie.

Jean shut the front door and put the baby back on the bed of the Morrison shelter. 'You little rascal! How did you manage that? Have you been holding out on us?' she admonished Janet, laughing.

'Now you have sorted her out we'll sit and watch her from the kitchen, and you can finish telling me about how you feel about Alan,' Florrie suggested.

'Like I said, Alan makes me laugh and he's not too serious about life. Don't get me wrong, he is serious about his job, but not in himself. Does that make sense to you?' Florrie nodded then Jean continued. 'In fact he is very ambitious. Since he had this last promotion he wants to get as far ahead as he can.'

'Mmm,' Florrie murmured. 'What are you going to do if Tom is still alive?'

Jean shrugged her shoulders. 'I don't really know what to do for the best. The trouble is that I still love both of them – but in different ways, like I said before.'

'But if it comes down to a choice, and it will, which one will you choose?'

'That is the trouble. I know I have to choose. But which? Tom or Alan? I don't expect you to answer that. Only I can.' Jean was in an obvious dilemma which only she could sort out. 'I will let you know when I've made my choice.'

Chapter Thirteen

It was not too long before Jean had to make the choice: only a matter of weeks.

As the school summer holidays were still on, Florrie and Jean had decided to take the children for a picnic over on the other side of the river to what they called 'their spot', opposite the cottages. Florrie was going to swim over and Jean, with Florrie's clothes and the picnic gear that the boys would help with, was going by ferry.

She was just getting the baby ready when Jeff called out that the second post had arrived. She told him to put it in the bag with Aunty Florrie's clothes – she would sort it out later.

Jean gathered the children together and walked down to Winter's Bridge and turned into Ferry Road to catch the one o'clock ferry.

On the way she met quite a few people who knew her and they all spoke to her and the children. She had to excuse herself without being rude, and told them she had to catch the one o'clock ferry. They all understood and they said it was a nice day for a picnic and to have a lovely time.

Florrie was waiting for them on the other side as the ferry pulled in. She took the bag from Jean that contained her clothes and the picnic basket from Michael. That left the boys free to run on ahead, and Jean to carry Janet.

Looking at Janet Florrie said, 'Wasn't it funny that day when Mr Taylor brought her in after she got out the front door.'

'Yes it was. But it scared the life out of me. She is a funny little thing. And the way she gets around like that is amazing. She even goes to the front door to pick up the post when it comes, and the milk,' laughed Jean. It was strange to Jean as Janet didn't crawl in the conventional way on all fours, but on her bottom, pushing her little legs out and then pulling them back. She could scoot along quite fast like that.

'You little love,' Jean said to Janet, blowing raspberries on her little hands as she carried her along.

'By the way, my second post is in your bag Florrie. I hope you don't mind. It came when I was getting ready.'

'No. Of course not. Don't you want to look at it?'

'No. Not yet thanks. There's probably nothing important there anyway.'

They walked along in silence for a while until Michael came running along the bank back toward them.

'What on earth is he wearing on his chest?'

Jean who had better eyes than Florrie burst out laughing and said, 'If I am not mistaken it looks like a brassiere.'

'Well I never. I wonder if it is the one I left here the last time we had a picnic?'

By this time Michael was upon them and he was laughing and posing saying to them, 'Look what I found in the bushes Mum, Aunty Jean.'

'You give that to me, you little devil, and let me look at it.' She was laughing at him then Jeff and Ken came to join them, not wanting to miss any of the fun.

'It is my brassiere, Jean! Thank heavens I've got that back. I didn't expect to see it again. Thank you Michael,' pulling him toward her and giving him a kiss.

She started to put it in her bag when she saw Jean's mail in there. 'Hello. What's this one here? It looks rather important, Jean.'

'Let me see.' She took it from Florrie's hand and turned it over in hers and said, 'It is from the War Office, Florrie. I wonder what it says. You open it please. I'm too nervous,' Jean said, going pale with fright.

'Give it here. But let's sit down first.'

They sat down in their usual spot and Florrie asked the boys to go and play. Janet sat pulling up daisies from the ground. Florrie started to open it the letter. 'Are you sure you don't want to read it yourself?'

'No. Just read it please.'

'Now let's see,' tearing open the envelope. She looked across at Jean in case she had changed her mind, but she had not, so she continued. She scanned the first few lines and let out a yelp. 'It's Tom! It's Tom! He's alive. He's alive! It says here that the Red Cross found him, then it goes on to say he is well and where he is. Oh, that is great news.'

They were both crying and laughing at the same time. At this, the boys came up to them asking what was the matter. And that made Jean laugh a bit louder and pulled Jeff and Ken toward her and told them that she has heard that Daddy is alive and well.

'Will he be coming home now?' asked Jeff.

'I'm afraid not, darling. He is in what they call a Prisoner of War camp, and he has to stay there until this nasty war is over.'

'Oh,' said Jeff. 'Can't we go and see him there then?' he asked hopefully.

'No, Jeffery. He is in another country across the sea. And no one is allowed to travel across the sea in these times,' Jean explained patiently to him. Jeff and Ken went off to play with Michael. Jeff looking thoughtful.

'I am so pleased for you Jean.'

'Thanks. I am pleased as well.'

Jean had some of the colour back in her cheeks and she just sat there staring.

'Come on Jean. Pass that Thermos flask over and let's have a cuppa to celebrate. Pity we haven't anything stronger,' laughed Florrie. Then she had a sobering thought which she spoke out loud asking Jean, 'Have you made up your mind about Alan yet?'

'No. That's what I was thinking about just then. I am afraid I've been putting it off. It's obvious that I can't put it off any longer. But what do I tell him?' asked Jean, not waiting for or expecting an answer.

★

The following evening when the children were asleep in bed Alan came around to the cottage.

They made love with their usual lack of inhibitions even though Jean felt guilty as always especially with what she had to tell Alan. She couldn't help herself.

Alan noticed that Jean was quieter than usual and he said as much to her.

'I know, and I am sorry. It's just that... it's just that... Oh, hell! I can't say this...' Alan stopped her with a kiss then said, 'If it is bad news just come out and say it. The same if it is good news. Now come on and tell me what is so important.'

'Tom is alive.' Silence. She repeated it. 'Tom is alive.'

'I heard you the first time,' whispered Alan. 'Where does that leave us?'

Jean could hear the pain in his voice. That brought tears to her eyes. What could she say to him. She knew what she had to say, but she couldn't speak.

'For God's sake Jean. Where does that leave us? Speak to me,' he said, choking the tears back.

'Oh I don't know,' said Jean in frustration. 'I told you at the beginning I would never leave Tom. I never expected this affair to go as far as it has.'

'But you love me, Jean.'

'But I love Tom as well. And I can't just write and tell him I want a divorce. Don't you understand that?'

'Why not? If you love me like you say you do, you can divorce him.'

'I can't do it Alan. I can't.' By this time they were both crying. 'I still love him, Alan, and I can't write and tell him I want a divorce. It wouldn't be fair to him or the children. He hasn't done anything to deserve it.'

'But it's fair to me for you to just say, "Thank you very much Alan. I enjoyed the slap and tickle when I thought Tom was dead, but he's alive now, so ta-ta." Is that fair, Jean?'

She was so shocked and hurt that she slapped his face with all the strength she could muster. 'Oh that's not fair Alan. That's not even worthy of you. I told you at the beginning that I would never leave Tom. And I am not going to.' He grabbed her wrists before she could slap him again. 'That doesn't stop me loving you, even though Tom is still alive. We can carry on the way we have been, Jean,' he pleaded.

'Stop it, Alan. Stop it, please. I am so sorry. I wish this had never happened. No I don't, for it has meant as much to me as I am sure it meant to you. But I am sorry. It can't continue. Can we still be friends?'

'Friends. Ha! That is asking too much, even of me, Jean. What do you expect me to do when I pass you in the street and knowing what we meant to each other. Ignore you? Or in the pub collecting the Club money. Ignore you?' The tears were running slowly down his cheeks. 'No Jean. I can't do that.' He reached for her then and softly kissed her.

With a sob she fell into his arms. He made love to her, this time even more tenderly than before. He kissed her tears away and gently kissed her on the lips. Everything about his lovemaking to Jean was as if it was the last time that he would ever make love to a woman. He would not let Jean participate at all. When she tried to take any initiative, he forestalled her by grabbing her wrists again but more gently than he had before. Her excitement was increasing, but still he would not let her do anything. So she just lay experiencing one joy after another.

His lips and tongue were all over her again and when his tongue reached that part of her that was extremely sensitive she just exploded with passion and shuddered to a climax. Alan still carried on caressing her and he soon had her aroused again. At last he entered her and with a long loud groan he released all the pent-up emotion that was within him.

All night long they made love to each other. Sometimes she made love to him, and sometimes he to her. But every time, they always seemed to reach heights that neither one of them had ever reached before, or even knew existed.

At long last they fell into an exhausted sleep.

When Jean awoke the next morning Alan was gone.

Chapter Fourteen

Alan had gone. Not only was out of her bed, but he was out of her life as well, although she didn't find this out until the Friday when she and Florrie went to pay the Club money.

There were times when she did not see Alan for nearly a week because he had to go up to London or South to Portsmouth on business, so she was not unduly worried that she had not seen him for a few days.

On Friday night when Bill Fowler came to collect the Club money she nearly fainted with shock when he addressed the lounge bar.

'Have you heard what Alan Armstrong's bin and gone and done?' Jean could not wait to hear but did not want to ask, but Florrie asked. 'Go on, tell us Bill, put us out of our misery.'

'He's gone and joined the Navy. The Royal Navy! He has been accepted, and as an Officer too. His Mum is ever so proud of him.'

'I thought he was in a reserved occupation,' one of the old chaps cried out.

'He is. Was, but he just went off to the Kingston Recruiting Office and spun them a yarn and they accepted him. He is now Sub Lieutenant Armstrong, Royal Navy. He went to Portsmouth yesterday to start his training,' said Bill.

All this time Jean was listening to Bill numb with shock, and she could not take any more. She just got up and pushed her way through the throng and out the door.

'Blimey. What's wrong with her?' asked Bill.

Florrie, trying to cover for her friend said, 'She must have eaten something that doesn't agree with her. I'll go and see if she's all right.'

When Florrie got to Jean's house, Jean was sobbing her heart out. She looked at Florrie and said, 'I didn't mean for him to go away and to join up.'

'You made up your mind between Alan and Tom, then.'

'Yes. I told him that night of the picnic, and I asked him if we couldn't be friends instead.'

'Instead of what Jean? Instead of being lovers? What did you expect? Did you think he would stay around and suffer every time he saw you Jean? No. He's done the only thing he could do. The only decent thing. And that is leave for a while until both of you have got over each other.'

'Who's side are you on Florrie?' The tears were still streaming down Jean's face.

Florrie went to Jean and held her in her arms. 'I'm on your side of course. But you have to be practical, Jean. I know you love Alan, but you have made the right decision in choosing Tom. After all, he is your husband the father of your three lovely children. And they are lovely, Jean.'

Jean looked up with tears still in her eyes and said, 'Thank you Florrie.'

'But as it is, Alan has gone and I am rather glad in a way. No... no, hear me out,' as Jean tried to interrupt her. 'Things were getting much too heavy for both of you. I was scared for you in case someone found out and told Tom. Could you imagine how he would feel, eh? Not being able to do anything from wherever he is. You needed some breathing space and Alan has taken the bull by the horns and given you some. He's joined up. And that's that.'

'But the Royal Navy! I can't bear the thought of it.'

82

'Don't think about it. Alan will be all right, Jean. He's one of those chaps who if they fell in a sewer would come up smelling of roses.'

'That is not fair Florrie,' said Jean, smiling in spite of herself. 'He's not like that at all.'

'No. I know. I was only kidding. But at least it made you smile. Now wipe your eyes and blow your nose and lets try and get back to like things were before Alan.'

'I am sorry. You must have felt so left out of things when I was with him. I am sorry,' she apologised once again.

'I did, but I knew you would come to your senses sooner or later. I'm just sorry that you had it so bad for Alan. It wasn't until tonight that I realised just how far things had gone and how much he meant to you.'

'Even I can't understand how I can still love Tom and be so in love with Alan. I am afraid I hit him that last night.'

'Good Heavens. Why?'

'It was something he said that really hurt me. The whole goodbye scene was fraught with anger and apologies.' Jean had tears in her eyes as she thought of that evening, and then she thought of what happened after the slap. She got up and turned her back so that Florrie wouldn't see her face, and put the kettle on.

'I'd hate to think what our stomachs will be like after all this tea. As long as this war doesn't go on much longer we still have a hope of not getting too addicted to it,' Jean said, changing the subject.

'I'll tell you what,' said Florrie, 'I've some of that Camp coffee indoors, if you like we could have some for a change.'

'Yes please. I'd like that. I can't remember the last time I had a cup of real coffee though. The Camp coffee will definitely make a change from tea,' Jean said wistfully.

'I'll pop into Mrs Mitchell's and thank her for baby-sitting then come back with the Camp coffee. I won't be a tick.'

Whilst Florrie was gone Jean tidied herself up and went upstairs to check on the boys. They were well tucked in and fast asleep. Janet was asleep too in her second drawer of the chest, her thumb in her mouth. 'Before you get much bigger my love we'll have to get a cot for you, won't we?' Jean said aloud. She went back down and started getting the cups and saucers ready for the coffee, and got out a bag of broken biscuits.

They both loved the broken biscuits that they got from Sainsbury's in Surbiton. Apart from being cheaper there was such an assortment in the bag. They kept the whole biscuits for visitors and the kids.

Florrie was soon back with the bottle of coffee. The kettle had boiled and soon they were sitting drinking coffee and dunking biscuits.

'It's just like old times,' said Florrie.

'I am sorry for all that's happened Florrie. I didn't realise how much...'

'Sssh. Don't apologise anymore. Just put it down to experience. You're only young once and you have made the most of it. Now let us both put it behind us and get on with our lives.'

Jean leant across the kitchen table and squeezed Florrie's hand.

They drank their coffee in companionable silence. Eventually Florrie said, 'How about we wrap the children up warm and take them to Hampton Court tomorrow?. What do you say?'

'Oh yes! We haven't been there for what seems like ages. And I agree with wrapping the children up warm – although the weather has been nice and sunny, it is getting a bit chilly. Just like autumn. I don't know how you could have swum across the river last week.'

'At least Michael found my bra for me!' At this they both laughed, and Florrie continued, 'It was practically brand new. It had only been washed once before I lost it.'

'A bit careless don't you think?'

'Yes, but we were rushing to catch the ferry home. I thought I had collected all my clothes and put them in the bag.' They were both having a chuckle over the lost bra.

'I did offer to go over and have a look for it for you.'

'Yes I know. Thanks. Something cropped up and you never went. Still, it doesn't make any difference what the reason was. At least I've got it now. I thought I'd lost that for good.'

'Say, I've got some powdered egg in the cupboard. How about some scrambled egg on toast?' Jean suggested.

'You can't use that up on me.'

'Hark who's talking! What about that tin of ham and that cake? Anyway, they took pity on me down at the Dairy and that Mr Peters gave me three extra fresh eggs, "For the kiddies," he said with a wink. Fortunately there was no one else in there. It would have caused a riot if there had been.'

'Most of the men take pity on you and the children. Look at those chaps from the Perspex factory, they spoil you rotten. They often drop off some little thing for either you or the children.'

'I know, and I feel awful about it. Half the time I don't know who it is, they just leave the goodies in the basket Tom fixed up on the handlebar of the pram. I feel as though it is a begging basket.'

At this Florrie laughed, and Jean started to mix up the egg powder with a little milk and water. Florrie was pleased to see that Jean was recovering her sense of humour.

Chapter Fifteen

It was the morning of Monday December 8th, 1941, when Jean heard on the radio news that the Japanese had attacked Pearl Harbour the previous morning. It was a sneak attack: the Mitsubishi Zero aeroplanes were the cause of nearly all the damage that was done. They also attacked the Army Air Force planes at Hickham and Wheeler airfields, the aircraft still on the ground.

The United States Navy were caught completely by surprise with many capital ships in harbour. Several were sunk, including three battleships. They capsized another and damaged four more, and many other vessels were seriously damaged. As there was no warning there was a serious loss of life; it being a Sunday morning, most of the ships' crews were having a well-earned rest. It was fortunate that none of the aircraft carriers were in harbour.

Not all this information was on the first broadcast Jean heard; it came in dribs and drabs in subsequent broadcasts and newspaper reports, and most people were able to put the pieces together.

Jean wondered if this would mean that the United States of America would join in the war on Britain's side. Britain could certainly use their help now that France had capitulated. Fortunately they had the help of Australian, New Zealand and many other Commonwealth volunteers, but with the USA on Britain's side, they had more than just a fighting chance.

She could not wait to discuss it with Florrie, but knew it would have to wait until the evening. Florrie had gone to visit an old aunt of hers.

When she told her the news Florrie was shocked, and then asked where Pearl Harbour was. Jean said that it is in the Hawaiian Islands in the Pacific, about halfway between the West Coast of the USA and Japan. Jean got her old school atlas out and showed Florrie on the map.

'Do you think the Americans will enter the war now?' asked Florrie.

'That's what we've been hoping for. Perhaps now that President Roosevelt has had a drop of our medicine he'll consider it. I hope they will come into it. With any luck it will shorten the war quite a bit if they do.'

'We'll have to wait and see. I am afraid the accumulator needs recharging so I can't listen to my radio. I'll have to take it down to get it charged the next time I go down the Bridge.'

'It's just coming up to news time in a few minutes.' Jean looked at her watch. 'Yes, we can listen to it while we have a cup of tea.'

There was nothing new on the news so they did not pay much attention to it. Just left it on in the background in case there was something important at the end. There was not, so Jean turned it off to save the battery.

★

The Americans entered the war and soon they appeared to be everywhere. Florrie and Jean saw some in Kingston when they went there a month or so after Pearl Harbour. They looked well-fed and very young. And most of them were. The young girls, and some not so young, were all over them.

The ordinary British serviceman did not like their presence at all. There was quite often friction between the two nationalities, especially at dances. The British accused the 'Yanks' of stealing their girls, and the Americans took exception. Many fights broke out over this, so it kept the Military Police busy.

Jean or Florrie were not bothered by them; they were polite to the young men and the Americans were equally polite in return. Neither of them had ever met an American so it made no difference one way or the other to them. And it didn't cost them anything to be polite.

Jean met a couple of young American officers on the train when she was taking Janet up to London to meet Jean's father. They seemed like nice chaps and they got talking to Jean. They really made a fuss of Janet. During the conversation it came up that Jean had two little lads as well, and the Americans took from their pockets photographs of their wives and families. Jean made the appropriate comments about their families. They asked where her husband was, and said that they were sorry about him being a prisoner of war.

The train journey was over very soon as it was only a short hop up to Victoria Station from Surbiton. On parting both officers gave Jean some chocolate for the children. Jean thanked them and wished them well.

Jean's father lived within walking distance of Victoria Station so she set off at a brisk pace, as brisk as she could carrying the baby.

She was soon at Old Pye Street where her father lived in a block of flats. Her mother had died in 1936, not long before Jeff was born. Now her father lived on his own except when one of Jean's brothers, Len, who still lived at home was on leave. Her other brother, Ted, was married and lived over in north-west London. That was difficult to get to, so she didn't get to see him and his family as often as she would have liked.

Len, her unmarried brother, happened to be on leave when Jean arrived. It was the first time either her father or brother had seen Janet and they really made a fuss of her.

Jean was pleased to see them both as she had not been home very much since the beginning of the war. If Florrie hadn't volunteered to have the boys for her she would not have been able to visit.

Florrie had persuaded her to stay the night at her father's as she could manage the boys on her own without any problems.

It really was nice for Jean to spend time with Len and her dad. They talked and talked about the war, about Tom, about her other brother, Ted, and his family and about her mother, whom Jean and her brother and father missed terribly.

Jean got to bed about eleven o'clock and it seemed like five minutes later, and not two hours, that there was that awful sound of the air-raid siren. Jean carried Janet, and Len helped their father along to St James's Park underground station which was being used as an air-raid shelter. It was far safer than ordinary shelters.

There was a warm feeling of camaraderie in the shelter. A lot of the folk down there knew each other or had got to know each other from using the same underground station since the beginning of the blitz.

Jean saw old friends of her mother's who greeted her as a long lost friend and asked after the family. As usual there was a very friendly atmosphere down there and it was not too long before someone started up a singsong with all the old songs from World War I, as it was being called now, and some from this war, and some between the wars too. Someone joined in with a piano accordion and someone else with a harmonica. It seemed like they were having a party down there. There was always someone down there who had a fantastic voice that you could hear over and above everyone else.

Strangely, Jean was not at all claustrophobic down in the underground, probably because it was large and airy. The shelter outside the City Arms was very small in comparison, and always felt chilly and damp.

Sitting on a rug with her back against a wall she closed her eyes and started thinking about Tom. She had often come here to meet him when he came over to see her. He had come from east London so it was easier for him to meet her at the St James's station entrance, then decide where to go on a date. It saved time too.

She had met Tom when he had come to the flats to see a friend. On the way out, on the stairs, he had bumped into Len, whom he knew only slightly. Len had just been to the off-licence to get some beer for himself and Jean's father. Seeing Tom, Len had asked him in for a beer, and had introduced him to Jean who unfortunately had a cold so she wasn't at her best.

Tom was ten years older than Jean. He was quite short for a man, only five foot five inches tall, about the same height as Jean, so Jean did not wear high heels when she went out with him. He had a rather forceful character and was quite used to getting his own way. That was not so surprising when one considered he was eldest of nine children. He tried to boss Jean around but she wouldn't take any notice of him, in fact, she just laughed at him. But he had piercing blue eyes that could stare anyone down. Jean found that out quite soon in their relationship.

Despite this, she fell in love with him. They got married on Christmas Day, 1935.

Len noticed Jean smiling to herself and asked what she was smiling at. She said, 'Do you remember that time when you first introduced Tom to me?' Len nodded his head and

Jean continued, 'He thought I was in the Salvation Army. He often tells people that when they ask us how we met. He always says, "I thought she was in the Salvation Army, sitting there oiling the sewing machine." The fool!'

'What made him say that?'

'Well, do you remember that red silk blouse I had that I had embroidered? I was wearing it with a navy blue suit. That's probably why he thought I was in the "Sally Ann". At a glance he mistook it for their uniform.'

'Where does the bit about you oiling the machine come into it then?'

'That's just a joke really,' laughed Jean. 'I had a stinking cold when you introduced him to me, and he always says that I had a runny nose and that I was oiling the machine. The bloody fool.'

'How awful of him to say that,' said Len, laughing as well.

'Jean! Watch your language,' her father ordered.

'Sorry Dad,' Jean apologised, still smiling.

They all sat quietly with their own thoughts and the noise of the other occupants sometimes broke in to their reveries. Her father lit his pipe and gently puffed away, Len tried to sleep, Janet was already sleeping and Jean sat there still thinking of Tom and Alan.

She had heard nothing of Alan since he had joined the navy in September. Not a whisper. She had tried very hard to forget him but it was very difficult as so much had happened. She did not know why she had been so willing to go to bed with him, for she was not a promiscuous woman. The only other person she had gone to bed with was Tom. She had been a virgin when they had married, so it was against her nature to be like that. There was something about Alan that was very persuasive, something about his eyes that she just could not resist. She found them mesmerising.

The song that was being sung at the moment intruded in on her thoughts. It was one of Jean's favourites, rather appropriately, 'Till we meet again'. Tom or Alan, or both?

She would have to make the same hard decision as she had made back in September with Alan, and this time it would be even harder.

She was pregnant again.

Chapter Sixteen

Len came home with her to stay for a few days as he had another week before he had to report back to his unit.

The boys were pleased to see him and he seemed pleased to see them. It was nice for them to have a man about the house for they were so used to the female company of Jean and Florrie.

He took all the children out for walks, and made it seem like they were adventures. It left the two women to relax and natter without being interrupted by one of the children asking them a question or wanting something.

Florrie could not hold back her question any longer. She had been meaning to ask it since before Jean went up to see her father. One day they were sitting having a cup of tea, and she just came out with it.

'Are you pregnant again, Jean?'

Jean was so surprised that she spluttered her tea all down her blouse. She looked up at Florrie, blushing.

'I can tell by your face the answer to my question. You are, aren't you Jean?'

Mopping at the tea as best she could, Jean told Florrie that she was.

'Oh my God! Not again.'

'This time it is more difficult to cope with, because it obviously isn't Tom's. You and I know whose it is, and you can imagine the meal that will be made about it all over Long Ditton with them all speculating which of the men is the father.'

'Heck yes. I can see your predicament. It's too late to try and do anything about it – with Alan having gone in September, that's nearly five months. What are you going to do this time? Fortunately you don't show yet, but you will do soon.'

'This time I'm just not sure. I could go to my dad's place, but I could lose the cottage if I stayed there, and anyway, Dad hasn't any room for us although he would manage somehow. He wouldn't turn me out. I know he's not well. He hasn't picked up since my mother died. So that can't be considered. I definitely can't go to Tom's family. Ted, my brother, has three kids of his own, so he's out too. I think I will have to hibernate indoors here and pretend that it's the "second immaculate conception"!'

'Jean!' said Florrie shocked. 'Don't be so irreverent.'

'I am sorry, Florrie. I shouldn't have said that, but I would like to keep this child. I felt so guilty about trying to lose the last one. I am glad it turned out okay, thank heavens.'

'I know. And Janet is a little treasure, isn't she.'

'Yes,' said Jean, smiling at the pleasure that all of her children had brought her. 'But this isn't getting me any closer to a decision of what to do. What can I do?' she asked the room in general.

Florrie was sitting drinking her tea very thoughtfully. Suddenly she said, 'I know...'

'What? Tell me, Florrie. What?' She was ready to jump at any suggestion, however silly it might be.

'Do you remember just before Christmas that letter you had from the authorities about evacuation?'

'Yes.'

'And you said that you wouldn't consider it... well you could go and be evacuated!'

'Florrie,' said Jean hugging her, 'what a good idea. But how does one go about that? I turned them down once. Surely it is too late now?'

'Have you still got the letter?'

'Yes, somewhere.'

'Well, go and find it and I'll start to concoct a letter to them telling them a sob story. Go on Jean,' Florrie said pushing Jean out of the room. 'Scoot!'

Whilst Jean was over at her place Florrie got out a scrap of paper, and started writing.

> *Dear Sir,*
>
> *I am awfully sorry to bother you, but in December when I declined your kind offer for myself and the children to be evacuated, I thought that there was hardly ever danger down here.*
>
> *Well, since then I have changed my mind due to the fact that I went up to visit my father in London and whilst there, there was a very serious Air-Raid causing extensive damage and so on and so forth...*

Jean came back with the letter about evacuation and Florrie showed her the letter she had written in rough.

Reading it Jean said laughingly, 'That's great Florrie, I'll use it in that form without the so ons and so forths.'

'I didn't mean for you to write that bit, you fool.'

'I know you didn't. I was just kidding.'

'Oh... so you like it then. You will have to add a bit more sob stuff but I am sure you can manage that – being an "edificated" lady,' she joked, using an expression that she had heard someone on the bus use once.

'That still doesn't solve the problem of what to do about the baby. I'll just have to grin and bear it so to speak for now. Excuse the pun, Florrie.'

'Don't let's worry about that now. Let's get the letter written and posted and see what the authorities say.'

*

The authorities came up trumps. They said she could go as soon as they found a family in the country who would take them in.

Two weeks later they got back to Jean and told her that she would be going to Nottingham the following Monday. Jean was so excited that she dashed over to Florrie's straight away.

Florrie was pleased for her but at the same time sad. She would miss her friend when she went. In fact she would be quite lonely without her and the children. And Michael would miss the boys, his playmates, too. She said as much to Jean and they both started crying.

'This is silly. Two grown women crying over nothing really, just a little separation,' said Jean.

'I know, but how long will it be?'

*

Jean left early Monday morning as it was quite a journey. She had changed the railway warrant on Sunday so that there would not be a mad rush on Monday morning.

Florrie and Michael came to see them off. When the train moved off there were tears in both women's eyes. They were waving to each other and Florrie was telling Jean not to forget to write. Jean promised she would as the train started to pick up speed.

'Bye.'

'Goodbye.'

They waved until they were out of sight of each other.

*

Jean and the children arrived at Nottingham in the early evening. They were met by a well-meaning female councillor and taken to the home of the family that would be putting them up.

The councillor asked all the usual questions.

'Did you have a nice journey? What is the bombing like in London?' She did not give Jean a chance to answer. In fact she was not at all receptive. Every time that Jean started to ask a question she was interrupted and the question was never answered. It struck Jean that the woman liked the sound of her own voice. Jean gave up trying to communicate with her.

At least the hoity-toity female had a car, for Jean was certain that she would never have found the place on her own.

They eventually arrived at their destination. Jean got out of the car and the councillor helped her with the bags and the boys.

The family that she and the children were billeted with consisted of a husband and wife, their grown-up son, a daughter who was a cripple and the wife's father who was wheelchair-bound.

They made them welcome half-heartedly and the wife, Mrs Davis, asked for Jean's Ration Books. Jean was about to protest but gave in when she saw the woman's tight lips and piggy-looking eyes.

The hoity-toity woman left soon after making the introductions, and Jean did not blame her.

Jean and the children were shown to a room that seemed to be in the attic. It was obvious that they were all sharing the same room. Mrs Davis showed Jean the bathroom and toilet. Sheer luxury: indoor plumbing. 'We have breakfast at seven thirty,' she informed Jean. Then she left Jean and the children to their own devices.

Jean got the children ready for bed. The boys both said they were hungry but Jean couldn't do anything about it. She was hungry, too. She had none of the sandwiches left that Florrie had made for them, so she was not surprised that they were hungry.

Jean read them a story until they had settled down, which fortunately did not take long. When they were all asleep she sat on the side of her bed and thought. She didn't think she would like staying there, that was for sure, but she was stuck with it so she would have to make the most of it.

Finally she decided to get into bed and try to sleep. It took longer than she thought, considering how tired she was.

The next morning she had the children up and dressed long before seven thirty. She didn't want to start off on the wrong foot on the first day by being late.

Breakfast consisted of an egg, a strip of bacon, and toast and jam. The bacon came as a surprise to Jean, especially as the boys were given some too. Perhaps she had done Mrs Davis an injustice. Jean soon changed her mind when the wife asked Jean what she was going to do all day; she did not want them hanging around the house. Jean was very angry, but held her temper. She answered, 'I don't know really. What is there to do around here?'

The wife said, 'You could go for a walk in the forest with my father and my daughter Agnes.'

Jean was a bit taken aback by this but she tried not to hesitate too long before answering. 'Yes, of course.'

The father, Mr Smith, was a real dear, not a bit like his daughter, and he took Janet on his lap and Jean pushed them both in the wheelchair. Jeff and Ken walked along with the daughter. Even she was nice away from her mother's influence.

The father showed Jean the way to Sherwood Forest, of Robin Hood fame. He told her a bit about the legend of Robin Hood and Maid Marion. He also pointed out places of interest for her. It was a chilly, but nice and bright day in late February.

Agnes, although crippled by poliomyelitis and having to wear callipers on both legs for support, played ball with Jeff and Ken as best she could and they really enjoyed themselves. She was quite chatty with the boys and soon had them laughing. Jean began to think that she might enjoy this stay after all, but how wrong could she have been...?

Chapter Seventeen

Florrie went over to Jean's to check on the place most days, to open the blinds and windows to give the place an airing.

Two weeks after Jean had left for Nottingham, she was most surprised to find Jean's bags on the floor in the front room. She inwardly cheered and instantly went to kitchen to put the kettle on.

While it was boiling she went back to her own home to get some powdered milk as she had no fresh milk left.

She returned and tried not make too much noise getting the cups and saucers out of Jean's cupboard. The kettle boiled so she made the tea. When she had gone to get the milk she brought some biscuits back with her.

She poured a cup of tea for Jean and put some whole biscuits on the saucer and started up the stairs to Jean's bedroom. Typically, the stairs creaked. Why is it, she asked herself, that stairs always creak when you are trying to creep around? It was the same in church, there was always something or someone that makes one laugh, and the harder one tries to stop laughing the worse it gets. The stairs were creaking like mad by the time she got to the bedroom, but she need not have worried, as Jean would not have heard her: she was dead to the world, sprawled across the bed.

Florrie gently shook her. It took some time before Jean reached consciousness, which was very slowly. When she eventually surfaced she jumped out of her skin when

Florrie spoke. 'Come on, sleepyhead. Here's a nice cup of tea for you.'

'Florrie! It's you. You frightened the life out of me.'

'Am I that much of an ogre then?'

'Of course not. I just thought you were the wife.'

'Well, I'm not. Now tell me what time you got home last night and then tell me what you're doing home.'

'I got home about two thirty. The train I caught must have been the milk train as it seemed to stop at every little whistle-stop. The one from Nottingham wasn't much better. Anyway, I managed to get a lift from the station.'

'That was lucky,' said Florrie. 'How did you manage that?'

'There was this Senior Officer of the Home Guard on the train. For some reason he wasn't in first class.' Jean paused to take a sip of her tea.

This gave Florrie a chance to say, 'Hang on a minute while I get a cuppa too.'

'Right,' said Florrie, plonking herself on the bed with her tea. 'Carry on.'

'Well, this officer was in the carriage we were in and we got to chatting. Apparently he was going over to Bushy Park to do some inspecting. I don't know why he got out at Kingston though. Anyway, I was rather pleased that he did for he offered us a lift as it wasn't too much out of the way.'

'You were lucky, otherwise you would have had to walk from the station. Now tell me why you are home? I am pleased, though, as I missed you all.'

'I missed you too Florrie. By the way, did you get the letter I sent last week?' Florrie nodded then Jean continued with her tale. 'Come the night before last I'd had enough. I couldn't take the wife's snide comments any longer. What actually was the last straw was that afternoon when we all arrived home, well, we didn't call it "home". When we got back with her father and daughter, there she was with her cronies drinking tea. My bloody tea. I knew it was mine as it was Brooke Bond and she had left the packet out on the side. So I told her I'd have my ration books back and she could keep *my*, underlined, *my* packet of tea and that we would be leaving in the morning. I was so angry that I had to leave the room before she could answer. I was nearly in tears with the anger. Heaven knows what else of mine she had been using and entertaining her friends with. I more or less said that to her when she gave me my ration books back.'

'What did she say to that, the old boot?'

'Not much. What could she say? I checked the books in her presence and there were quite a few coupons missing. More than we would have used. At least she had the decency to blush. Especially as all this was going on in front of her friends.'

'I don't blame you for coming home.'

'Thanks. It's good to be home! I felt sorry for her father, for he seemed a lovely old boy, and was always grateful when we got back from the walks, a bit like my dad. He tried to persuade me to stay, but I couldn't. I'd had enough of it, I said. He said it would mean his daughter, the wife, wouldn't be allowed to take in evacuees, and that she would lose the allowance that she got for it.

I had reported her to the authorities and actually spoke to the hoity-toity councillor. They are going to take her off their lists. Ah, what a shame,' said Jean cynically.

'I should think so. What did you do for money to get you all home?'

'I still had some of the twenty pounds left, but hoity-toity gave me a railway warrant, so I didn't have to use my money. She actually offered us different accommodation, but I turned her down.'

'What are you going to do now?'

'Put the boiler on and have a non-regulation hot bath. Even though there was indoor plumbing, she was very stingy with the hot water for baths.'

'No. I didn't mean that. I meant about the baby,' asked Florrie.

'Oh that. I don't even mind the stigma of having it here. Anything is better than being up there.'

'I know it sounds selfish, but I'm glad you are back home.'

'Thank you, dear. I'm very glad to be here. How is Michael? And Joe, has he been home?'

'Yes, he was home last weekend. He had some good news too, he is being posted to Biggin Hill, so I'll be able to see more of him.'

'Oh, that is good news, Florrie.'

'Even though he was only in Scotland, it might well have been the opposite side of the world for all the amount of time I saw him. I know that Michael will be pleased to be able to see more of him.'

'Yes, I'd expect that. I just wish that Tom was home. God knows how long it will be before this damn war is over. The boys have seen their father, but Janet – the poor little thing – has never met him.'

'I know. I was just thinking that the other day.'

'Well this won't do. I had better get up and put the boiler on for this bath.'

'Tell you what,' said Florrie, 'why don't I take all the kids to my place so that you can have your bath in peace?'

'That would be lovely Florrie. Do you think you could give me a hand in with the tub then please?'

'Yes, of course.'

Florrie went to rouse the children to take them over to her place. Jean called out to Florrie that she would keep the bath water. When she had finished her bath she would put the kids in and give them one as well.

'Okay. Yell out when you want them back. I'll give them some breakfast when I get back to my place.'

Jean pulled the blinds at the kitchen window then took her dressing gown and nightdress off. She stretched and sighed in anticipation of the bath. Then she stepped into the bath, sat down, and then lay back and relaxed.

She examined her growing belly. Fortunately it did not show too much, but within the next few weeks it would really be obvious that she was pregnant.

'Six months. Nearly six months since Alan joined the Royal Navy,' Jean thought to herself. 'I wonder if I'll ever see him again?' She lay in the hot water and thought about the times they had been together. Thinking back on the times they were together sexually, she couldn't understand why she had enjoyed the act so much. It was probably because Alan was more considerate of her feelings, making sure she was ready for him. Not like Tom, who only thought of himself and just carried on regardless of her feelings, except that last time when he had come home on embarkation leave. The difference between the two men in her life was unbelievable. Tom said he loved her and was very good and generous with them all, and strangely, she loved him in her own way.

Even though she was pregnant with Alan's baby, she still loved Tom, but she was beginning to think it was wrong to have sent Alan away like she did. She thought to herself, Oh what the hell! I just don't know what's right, and what's wrong any more. Give Tom up for Alan, or Alan for Tom? I love Alan too. I love them both.

Still in a quandary she started to wash herself. Having done that she dried herself and got dressed, she made a fresh pot of tea, then called over to Florrie's to say she had finished her bath and to send the kids over.

When Florrie brought the children over Jean told her that she had just made a fresh pot and asked her if she would like one.

'Have you ever known me to refuse a cup of tea?'

'Thinking about it, no.' Jean laughed. 'I must say I feel a lot more civilised for having had that bath. Oh. I only have the powdered milk at the moment. I hope you don't mind.'

'Of course not silly. Anyway, that is what I put in yours when I brought you that cup in bed.'

'I didn't even notice. Now come on boys, get undressed and into that bath.'

'Ooh! It isn't Friday yet Mum,' said Jeff.

'No, I know. But that train journey must have left some dirt on you. So don't argue and get undressed. I'll sort Ken and Janet out and you can all have a bath together.'

Michael asked if he could get in and Florrie looked across at Jean who nodded, and Florrie started to undress Michael. It was beginning to turn into a party.

'I'll just go and get Michael some fresh clothes,' Florrie said.

'Leave his dirty stuff here and I'll put his things in the copper with ours if you like. I'm putting the copper on again when I have finished washing these little scallywags.'

The children were having a grand time in the bath together. Jeff was washing Janet's face and Ken was trying to help him. She was laughing away enjoying all the attention she was getting.

They eventually finished the mass bath and when they were all dried off and standing glowing and clean, Jean asked them what they wanted to do today.

Michael said, 'Have a picnic,' but Florrie said it was too cold. Jeff said, 'Go to the pictures.' And that was what they decided to do.

Snow White and the Seven Dwarfs was showing again according to the paper. Jean said she'd do the washing the following day when the boys were at school.

Jean treated them all to the pictures. They all enjoyed the film, although Ken got a bit frightened when the wicked Queen appeared on the screen. Janet slept right through it all on Jean's lap.

They got home and all went to Jean's for tea. She had managed to pick up some bits and pieces for it when they were in Surbiton. It rounded off the day very nicely. Jean and Florrie had practically forgotten there was a war on, except they were reminded of it by the amount of food on the table, or lack of it.

There was enough to eat, but not a very good selection due to the rationing regulations. Jean and Florrie happened to look at each other and said in the same instant.

'Damn war!' they exclaimed, and laughed.

Chapter Eighteen

When Michael and Jeff were at school it was fairly quiet for Florrie and Jean with just Ken and Janet at home.

Even though the two little ones were on their own, it was surprising what mischief they got up to. One day Jean had gone upstairs to change the sheets on the beds and left Ken and Janet playing quietly. When she came back downstairs Janet had gone from being a white blonde-haired child to a black-haired one. Jean was furious more with herself than Ken. He had found the black lead polish in the kitchen which Jean used for blackleading the fireplace. She had forgotten to put it away. Ken and Janet thought it great fun. It took days to wash it out of her hair.

Another time, some months before the blacklead incident, Jean had been distempering the kitchen a pale shade of green and had gone outside to get the washing in as it was just beginning to rain. She was only gone a few minutes and when she had come back in Janet had pale green hair. Both Jeff and Ken got a good hiding for that and they were sent to their room in disgrace.

Fortunately Janet's hair was beginning to turn to light brown now, so it did not attract as much attention.

Because Florrie had no one at home during the day she was at a loose end, she spent most of her days through the garden at Jean's. Jean did not mind at all, and was in fact rather glad of the company.

They would spend the time chatting or reading. Sometimes Jean would be doing some alterations and Florrie would sit and talk to her; sometimes they would be listening to the radio. Inevitably they would be drinking tea.

In the afternoons, they would put their coats on and wrap the children up warm, and go to pick up Michael and Jeff from school.

It was a morning like any other morning in late March, when Jean received another letter from the War Office.

'What can it be this time?' Jean asked Florrie.

'I don't know. But there's only one way to find out.'

'Yes...' Jean's hands were shaking with fear as she tried to open the envelope. She had got it open and started to read it. Her face went as white as sheet and tears started forming in the corner of her eyes as she held out the letter to Florrie.

Florrie took it from Jean and started to read it. Her eyes filled with tears too and made it quite hard to read. But she finally read it.

Dear Mrs Drummond,

It is with deepest regret that the War Office have to inform you that your husband, Bombardier Thomas Albert Drummond, contracted pneumonia and after a prolonged illness died in January...

The letter went on to say that his personal effects would be sent on to her at a later date, and that he'd be sorely missed by the other men in the unit; that if there was anything they could do she should contact...

By the time Florrie had finished reading they were sobbing in each others arms.

The children, surprised at seeing their mummy and Aunty Florrie crying, started crying too. Jean held her arms out to them and they ran to her and hugged her. Not understanding anything, they soon got bored and went off to play.

Wiping her eyes Florrie said, 'I'll go and get the boys if you like and take Ken and Janet with me if you want to be alone.'

'No. I am all right Florrie, thank you. I should be used to this by now. At least I know for sure.'

'Are you sure you are okay? I'm quite willing to collect the boys on my own.'

'Yes I know you are, but I'll come with you. Perhaps the fresh air will clear my head,' said Jean wiping the rest of the tears from her eyes.

Florrie was a bit worried for she could remember the last time Jean had received a letter from the War Office. Perhaps, as Jean said, this was different.

They dressed the children in warm clothes and went up to Windmill Lane Primary School to meet Michael and Jeff.

On the way, in Windmill Lane, Jean's eyes strayed across to the waterbed that was damaged by a bomb. She felt guilty as her thoughts strayed to Alan. She wondered where he was, and if he was still alive. Not that it made any difference to her – their torrid love affair had ended last September.

They picked the boys up at the school and on the way back when they reached the Rec, the two women let the children play on the swings. Florrie asked Jean, 'Are you all right? You seem very quiet.'

'Yes. Fine thank you. I am just putting off going home because I'll have to tell the children of Tom's death. I don't think Ken will understand, and Janet definitely won't. But Jeffery, well that's a different story. Although he is older, he is very sensitive. I'm dreading it.'

They eventually got home from the Rec and Florrie said that she would go on home and leave Jean to it. But as she was about to leave Florrie said, 'Don't hesitate to call me if you need me.'

'Yes, I will, thanks.'

Jean took the children's coats off and hung them up. She coaxed some life back into the fire and told the children to come into the kitchen. Then came the bit she had been dreading. Telling the children.

When she was sure she had their attention she told them. 'Today I had another letter from the War Office.' This for Jeff's benefit. 'It said that Daddy is dead, but he died a hero.' Why did I say that? she thought. She awaited the outbursts of tears from them but none were forthcoming. 'Haven't you got anything to say?' she asked them.

Jeff seemed to be hesitating as though he was trying to formulate a question. Eventually he said, 'Mummy, I thought Daddy was safe in the prison camp, with no more fighting to do.'

'He was.' Jean hesitated before answering further. Then she went on, 'Although he was supposed to be safe in the camp, there are always things that you can die of.' She took a deep breath before she carried on speaking. 'Like sickness and disease. In Daddy's case he caught pneumonia and it was fatal. That means he died from it, Jeffery. Do you understand me?'

'Yes Mummy.' That was all he said. Jean worried that he was bottling everything up inside him, but what could she do but keep a close eye on him?

She started to get them their tea and the children went into the front room to play with the train set Tom had bought them.

Jean reflected on the days events and very quietly, so that the children would not hear her, she started to cry again. This will not do, she told herself. Pull yourself together, for the sake of the children. She did just that, and wiped her tears away and continued getting the tea.

'Come and get your tea,' she called to them in the front room. They came with Janet climbing up the steps between front room and kitchen on her hands and knees, then toddled unsteadily to her high chair. Jeffery helped her into it, then sat himself down.

'Oh good. Baked beans on toast. My favourite,' Ken said.

'I think it is a favourite for all of us,' said Jean.

They all tucked in. Jeff helped Janet cut up her toast. Strange really, that since her birth he seemed to think it was his God-given right to look after her, feeding and helping her along the way.

'If you have all finished your tea you can have an hour listening to the radio, then off to bed.'

Jeff had hardly spoken to anyone except when he was spoken too. He did everything that was to be done like an automaton. Jean would definitely have to watch him.

By seven o'clock they were all in bed. Jean had tucked them all in and kissed them good night. All three of them were in the same room above the kitchen, so Jean could hear if any of them got out of bed.

At about half past eight she heard movement above her head. Quickly she realised that she could hear Jeff come down the stairs. She recognised his tread. She went to the bottom of the stairs to see what he wanted.

He was sobbing and shivering. She grabbed a coat from the hook on the wall above his head and wrapped it round him. Jean supposed, correctly, that delayed shock had set in.

She led him to the kitchen and sat him down on a chair in front of the fire. When she started rubbing his feet that to her seemed nearly frozen, he stopped sobbing and just sniffed a couple of times, and then became silent.

'What's the matter, dear? Is it because of Daddy?'

'Yes. What are we going to do without him?'

'We'll just have to manage somehow. But all of you will have to help,' she told him. She had been thinking along those lines when she had heard his movement above her head. Being older than the other two it was obvious he would understand what was going on.

'Would you like some hot milk, Jeffery?' she asked, getting up to put some milk in a pan. He nodded and she turned the gas on under the milk. She sat back down in the chair beside him and continued to cuddle him. 'When the new baby is born I'll have to get a job to support us all. But that's not for you to worry about. As I have said, we'll definitely manage somehow,' she assured him.

Chapter Nineteen

After Jean and Florrie got back from taking Jeff and Michael to school, they were sitting in Jean's kitchen when Florrie asked Jean, 'How are you? Have you got over the shock of Tom's death?'

'I'm all right, I'm over the worst of the shock, thanks. I'm just numb now. But Jeff was upset last night, poor thing. It's strange really, I haven't cried much since I received the letter.'

'You've probably had enough to think about what with one thing and another.'

'Yes. I've been thinking of where we're going to live now that Tom is dead,' said Jean.

'I am sure that as long as you pay the rent you will be all right.'

'Yes. But that is just the problem. You see we were only able to rent this place from Watney's as Tom had a job with them.'

'Is that all that is worrying you? You needn't bother about that. Joe has never worked for Watney's, nor has Mr Reynolds next door to me. So like I said, as long as you pay the rent there won't be a problem. Don't worry about that Jean. You'll be okay.'

'Thanks Florrie. You've put my mind at rest. Now all I need to do is get this baby over with,' Jean said holding her stomach, 'and get a job to support us all.'

'Worry about that after you have had it. When is it due?'

'May or early June.'

It was only the end of March now so she had another two or three months to go. Or so she thought. Just a few days after hearing of Tom's death she went into premature labour.

Florrie called for an ambulance and went with Jean to the hospital. She couldn't stay with Jean because of the children. Mrs Mitchell was looking after Ken and Janet but she could not be expected to meet the other two from school.

As the baby was premature Jean had to stay in the hospital a bit longer.

Florrie managed to look after the children very well, and in fact rather enjoyed it. It was easier to look after them at Jean's house – it would mean too many changes for the younger children otherwise.

Jean's neighbours were helpful, even though they didn't approve of her new baby. They could do their sums too, and no way was this Tom's baby. But they were tolerant because they liked her, and so they forgave her. Mrs Mitchell guessed who the father was but she wasn't telling anyone.

*

Three and a half weeks later, Jean came home with the baby. It was surprising how well the baby had done. It seemed strong from the start and had no trouble surviving.

Jean had another little boy. He was the spit and image of Alan, but at least he had her eyes which were a very vivid blue. It wasn't likely that they would go dark now, she hoped: Alan's eyes were very dark, practically black. If he took after Alan in other things he would be a very hand-some child, but it was too early to tell if he had the same colour hair, since he didn't have any at all yet.

She wanted to call him Alan after his father but that was asking for trouble. Instead she named him after her cousin Philip.

The cottage was rather crowded with four children in the house. Jean had taken what was left of Tom's clothes out of the wardrobe and chest of drawers and taken them to the Salvation Army. She used one of the drawers for Philip to sleep in, as she had with Janet, but it was just as well she had kept the pram!

Despite keeping up with the dressmaking and alterations, and her small widow's pension, she still needed to find a job to make ends meet with her growing family.

She managed to get a full-time job, and although it seemed strange, she shared it with Florrie, which worked out well. It was only a cleaning job in a big house toward Surbiton. Jean and Florrie took each of the shifts in turn. Whoever did the afternoon shift came back the following day to do the morning shift. While one was working, the other looked after the children and their homes. It was hard work, especially for Jean, for she had four children to feed and wash and clothe while Florrie only had one. She preferred doing the morning shift but since that wasn't fair on Florrie, she didn't even broach the subject.

It was one of the afternoons in late 1943 when Jean was working that Florrie decided to take the children for a walk.

Ken had started the same school as Jeff and Michael in September, and so Florrie only had Janet and Philip with her. Philip was lying down, and Janet was sitting up with her legs over the back of the pram.

Florrie thought she heard a familiar voice call to her. She turned and found Alan Armstrong struggling through his mother's garden gate on crutches. She waited for him to catch up with her.

He held out his hand to her and asked how she was. Florrie took his hand and shook it and asked what had happened to him.

'Oh, this!' he said, looking down at his legs. 'I had an argument with a bit of shrapnel when we were on the Murmansk run to Russia.'

Florrie was curious to know how bad the damage was, but she didn't like to ask. Instead she said, 'You are looking well though, Alan. How's your mother?'

'She's doing very well, thank you.' He was looking at the pram and Florrie could almost see his brain working overtime, but she waited for him to speak. Eventually he said, 'Have you and Joe had another baby, Florrie? I guess this is Janet as she is just like Jean,' he said, tickling Janet under the chin. 'Hasn't she grown!'

'Yes she has, hasn't she?' said Florrie, prolonging the agony. 'No. Joe and I didn't have another baby.' At that moment Philip opened his eyes and then Alan knew.

'Good God!' he exclaimed. 'It must be Jean's. It has her eyes. What is it – a girl or boy?'

'A boy. His name is Philip. Jean wanted to name him after his father but she didn't like to as people would start speculating. They're probably doing that in any case though. Now, I must go and meet the boys from school.'

'Before you go, tell me please – how is Jean?'

'She is very well, considering she has four children to look after now.' Having said that she turned on her heel and walked off up Windmill Lane towards the school.

Chapter Twenty

When Jean arrived home she could tell something had happened but Florrie was not saying anything.

'Come on Florrie, tell me what has happened,' Jean pleaded with her.

'Not in front of the children, Jean.'

Jean looked around. Jeff and Michael were within ear-shot so Florrie still would not say anything. She could not wait for the children to be out of the way, so she started getting the tea ready for them all.

'You are rotten, Florrie Hunter! You just wait until there is something *you* want to know. You'll see how long I'll keep you waiting,' Jean said with a chuckle in her voice.

Florrie just smiled, and Jean gave up.

Tea finished, Jean got the children ready for bed. Florrie went to get Michael ready for bed and she said she would be over later.

When the children were in bed and she had read them a story she came back downstairs and started to clear away the tea things. She washed up and started to put away the children's toys. Twenty minutes later she put the kettle on and waited for Florrie.

She heard Florrie coming through the back yard. As soon as she was in the kitchen Jean pounced on her.

'Hang on. Hang on. Let me sit down first and get a cuppa.'

'I am sorry Florrie. But patience isn't one of my virtues, as you well know.'

'You're telling me! I'll put you out of your misery now. You'd never guess who I saw this afternoon?'

'Who? The King and Queen, Clark Gable? Come on tell me. Stop playing games. Please tell me,' pleaded Jean.

'Okay,' said Florrie, loving every minute of Jean's frustration. 'Alan Armstrong.'

Jean was dumbfounded when she heard. 'What did he look like?' she said, trying to play it cool.

'Like Alan Armstrong. Who else would he look like?'

'Ooh. You know what I mean.'

'Oh, "what did he look like".' Florrie was enjoying herself. 'He looked very handsome in his naval officer's uniform. He was coming out of his mother's house in Windmill Lane. He has two gold rings on his sleeves so he must be a very high-ranking officer.'

'He is a Lieutenant. What did he have to say?'

Laughingly Florrie said, 'He asked me if Joe and I had had another baby.'

'Whatever made him ask that?'

'How naive can you be. He saw the baby in the pram and assumed it was ours. I told him no, but didn't enlighten him as to whose it was. Alan would still be wondering if Philip hadn't opened his eyes. Then he knew it was yours, and he said as much. But I bet he is still wondering who the father is.'

'I am glad you didn't tell him that it was ours. His and mine I mean.'

'Why ever not?' Florrie cried out indignantly. 'He should shoulder some of the responsibility as well.'

'I don't want to hold a gun to his head and make him feel that he has to do something for me.' She paused for a moment and added worriedly, 'You didn't tell him about Tom, did you?'

'Don't be daft! Of course I didn't. As you haven't told anyone else except his family and close neighbours, I was certainly not going to tell Alan Armstrong that Tom was dead. That is up to you.'

'Thank you. I always seem to be thanking you for one thing or another.'

There was a knock at the front door. 'I wonder who that could be?' said Jean getting up.

The blackout curtains were drawn so she had difficulty seeing who it was. At first she thought it was a policeman. Then he spoke.

'Hello Jean. It's me. Alan.'

'Oh. Come in Alan.' She stood back to let him pass. She was surprised to see him on crutches. Florrie had not mentioned that to her. She adjusted the blackout behind him and followed him through to the kitchen.

'Hello again Florrie,' Alan said, struggling with the steps up to the kitchen.

'Hello, Alan.' To Jean she said, 'I had better be going, I've left Michael on his own.'

'Please don't go on my account Florrie,' Alan said. 'You haven't finished your tea yet.'

'No, don't go Florrie,' said Jean, not wanting to be alone with Alan. She offered Alan a cup of tea which he accepted. Eventually Jean plucked up the courage to ask him what happened to his leg.

'As I told Florrie this afternoon, I had an argument with a bit of shrapnel, and I came off worse.'

'Is it bad?' asked Florrie.

'Well not really. It depends on how you look at it. I've only half a foot left on my right leg.'

'Oh, how awful for you. Will it affect your walking much?' asked Jean.

'No, though it does at the moment, which is to be expected; but in the long run I hope it will get better.'

'I really must go Jean, as it is obvious you have things to talk about, so I'll be off. See you tomorrow Jean. Goodnight Alan.'

'Goodnight Florrie,' Jean and Alan chorused, getting up at the same time.

Florrie went out the back door of the kitchen. Jean followed her to adjust the blackout blind, but before she'd put the final bit of curtain down Jean said again, 'Don't go Florrie, please,' she whispered. Florrie smiled and said, 'Are you scared to be alone with him?'

'Yes.' Florrie just chuckled and went back to her cottage.

When Jean got back inside she found Alan had started to stack the cups and saucers ready for washing-up.

'Thanks Alan. You shouldn't have done that. I'll wash them in the morning.' She sat down and looked at the floor. She didn't know where to look or what to say.

Alan was quiet too. He took a packet of cigarettes out of his pocket and offered one to Jean who shook her head.

'Do you mind if I do, Jean?'

'No. Of course not. I'll find you an ashtray.' She found one in the front room. She put it in front of him and said, 'Why did you come here, Alan? I thought I'd made myself clear about not wanting to see you again, the last time you were here.'

'I wouldn't have, except that I saw that little boy in the pram.'

'So.'

'So it doesn't take a genius to see who's child it is.'

'How discerning of you Alan. You are correct. He is my child, as Florrie told you this afternoon.'

'Jean, please. Don't play games with me. I meant it is obvious that I am the father. Apart from the eyes, he's the spitting image of me when I was about his age. I am sorry Jean. Why didn't you let me know?'

'I didn't want to. And anyway, where would I have written to? You just breezed off with no goodbyes and no apologies, and after such a wonderful night.' Jean was blushing just with the thought of what happened that night.

Alan laughed at Jean's discomfort and said, 'I see you haven't changed, Jean.'

'What do you mean?'

'The blushing. It still doesn't take much to make you blush.'

Jean laughed for the first time since Alan had turned up that evening, and was still blushing.

'What are we going to do Jean, I mean about the baby?'

'It still stands, the way we left it the last time you were here.'

'But the baby is mine. How are you going to explain it to Tom? He's not stupid enough to ever think it is his.'

'Of course he's not,' said Jean angrily.

'Have you written to tell him that you have another child?'

For an answer the tears started rolling down her cheeks. Alan went to put his arms about her, but she pushed his arms away. 'No, Alan. Please, no.'

'But whatever is the matter Jean? Is it something I have said?'

'No, you haven't said anything wrong,' she said, wiping her eyes on the handkerchief he offered her, 'it's just that Tom is dead.'

'What! He can't be. You told me that he was alive and in a POW Camp,' Alan exclaimed. 'Now you tell me he is dead. How did you work that out?'

'He was alive that last time as I had said, but he died later of pneumonia. They told me in March last year.' This time she did not resist him when he put his arms around her. He tried to calm her down by rubbing her arms gently as if they were cold, and stroking her hair. And then he kissed her eyes.

Jean pulled away again when she felt him growing hard. 'We mustn't, Alan.'

'Why not? There is nothing to stop us now, or anyone.'

'No Alan. Please.'

For an answer he pulled her to him again. He kissed her hard on the lips. At first she did not return his kiss but as he got more persistent she gave herself up to him. Despite his wound, he lifted her into his arms and took her to the front room.

Why is it, Jean thought, that I can never resist him? Why should I? I still love him.

Alan stood her down and slowly with the help of light from the kitchen, he started to undress her. She started to undress him too but he stopped her when she got to his trousers. He held back.

'What's wrong Alan?'

'My foot.'

'Does it hurt?'

'A bit. But that's not the problem. It's not a very pretty sight. I don't want you to look at it.'

'Don't be silly, Alan. I am the mother of four and the sights I have seen should have prepared me for nearly anything. But I won't look at it if you don't want me to.'

'Thanks Jean.' With that he turned his back on her whilst he took off his trousers.

Jean could still see his foot even though he had his back to her. It was an angry red, not quite healed yet, but it wasn't at all how she thought it would be. Where the toes usually were the foot seemed to stop halfway between the ankle and the toes.

Alan turned suddenly and caught her looking at what was left of his foot. She blushed again when she was caught in the act of staring at it. She thought she ought to explain herself. 'It looks as though it is really healing nicely. How will it affect you walking?'

As she had seen it and it didn't horrify her they talked about his wound naturally. They sat in the bed and pulled the sheets and blankets up around their necks and just talked and talked. Trying to catch up with everything that had happened to them since they had last met.

'How long have you been smoking, Alan?'

'More or less since I joined the Navy. When they issue you with your uniform they give you some tobacco coupons. You can change them for either ready-made cigarettes or tobacco called "Tickler" in a tin, a bit like a cocoa tin, so that you could roll your own. It seemed a shame to give the coupons away. I find it calms the nerves.'

'What do you do in the Navy? I presume you have a trade.'

'Yes. I am the Gunnery Officer. That's how I got this.'

'What happened then?'

'One of the forward guns got hit when we were escorting a convoy to Murmansk, in Russia. I rushed forward to help the guns crew, when the whole thing exploded.' He shuddered as he thought of it.

'Don't talk about it if it's too painful.'

'No. It's all right Jean, although this is the first time I have really spoken of it. The ship was hit by two torpedoes. One amidships, and another for'd. It must have been the one that hit for'd that caused the magazine to blow up, in turn blowing up the for'd gun. God knows how I wasn't caught in the blast as I was only about fifteen feet away. A piece of metal just sliced half my foot off. I hadn't realised that that had happened as I didn't feel any pain at all. I was lucky really.'

'What happened to the guns crew?'

'They were blown to smithereens.'

Jean didn't say anything, but shuddered at the thought of those poor lads, and left Alan to his thoughts. How awful for him to have experienced that.

He drew Jean into his arms and kissed her gently. Eventually he spoke.

'Will you marry me Jean?'

She thought about his question and said, 'No, Alan. I am flattered to be asked. But I have four children and that's no way for you to start married life for the first time.'

'Jean, one of those children is mine, and I get on all right with the others.'

'Philip is no reason for you to want to marry me.'

'He is. He is my son. And I love you so much that I could have died when you sent me away last time. Listen to me Jean, please. Hear me out,' he said as she tried to interrupt him. 'I have a good job to go back to when this war is over. I have a large house that I rattle around in on my own. It has an indoor toilet and, best of all, a bathroom. I have some money that my father left me when he died. And as you well know I love you. What more could you want?'

'I love you too, Alan, but the reason I didn't tell you about Philip was because I didn't want you to feel trapped and feel you had to do something. But like I said earlier I didn't know where you were.'

'You could have asked my mother.'

'No Alan. I couldn't.' She went on to tell him about the trip to Nottingham and how she had hoped she could get away with having the baby there and coming back with a *fait accompli*, and tell all, if they asked, that she had adopted Philip. But as she was there only for about two weeks that didn't work out.

'Then why won't you marry me Jean? Those are only excuses. What are you worried about – the children? We can hold a vote for it with the children if you like.'

'I can't do that.'

'Why not? We can ask them in the morning. Now come here and stop putting barriers in our way.'

'But...' Alan stopped her protest with a kiss. He then started to make love to her, and all her protests flew out of the window as she experienced such joy.

They made love on and off all night, joyfully; it was not like the time before when they'd thought it would be their last.

Alan brought Jean to such exquisite heights that she hadn't believed were possible. At one point she was just about to climax when he asked her to marry him again.

'Yes. Oh yes...!' she panted as she climaxed.

Afterward she said that that was not fair to ask her at such a moment.

'At least you said yes. In fact a few times if I remember correctly,' he laughed.

'Oh... you!' she cried, and threw a pillow at him. 'Go to sleep and we will ask the children in the morning,' she said, smothering a yawn.

Chapter Twenty-One

Jean awoke and was surprised to find herself in the Morrison shelter bed. Then she remembered what had happened. She stretched luxuriously thinking about Alan's proposal.

'Come on, sleepyhead, time to get up. You have a big day before you,' Alan said, handing her a cup of tea.

'Thanks, that's just what I needed.' Taking a sip, she asked what time it was. When Alan told her she shot up in bed and banged her head on the steel top of the shelter. 'Ouch! That'll teach me not to rush first thing in the morning.'

'Are you all right Jean? You gave yourself a nasty bang on the head then.'

'I'll survive,' said Jean, rubbing her head.

'I found a new toothbrush in the cupboard over the sink. I hope you don't mind.' He leant over and kissed her.

'Mmm. No. You need a shave,' she said, rubbing his stubbly cheek. 'I can't help you with a razor, though.'

'Don't worry about it. I was thinking of growing a beard in any case.'

'Over my dead body!'

Alan laughed at the vehemence with which she had spoken. He knew then that she had accepted him. Now they only needed the children's approval.

'I had better get up and start to get the children up and ready for school.'

'If you like, tell me what you want for breakfast and I'll start to get it ready.'

'Thanks, Alan. I need to go out the back yard first.'

'That's one thing you won't have to do when you marry me,' he said smiling.

Jean smiled back at him but did not answer him. When she came back she was shivering. 'Brr. It's cold out there.'

'Another reason you should marry me.'

'Oh, shut up and pour me another cup of tea will you!' She went to wash herself at the kitchen sink.

He was watching her and strangely enough, she wasn't embarrassed at all. Another reason he thought she should marry him.

When she was dressed she went upstairs to get the children up. Jeff and Ken were already awake and went downstairs to wash before having breakfast.

When they got downstairs they were most pleasantly surprised to find Alan there.

'Hello Mr Armstrong,' said Jeff politely. Alan turned from the pot of porridge he was stirring and said, 'Hello Jeff, hello Ken. Are you hungry?'

'Yes thank you.'

Alan dished up two bowls of porridge and put them on the table. Jeff and Ken started to eat.

Jeff asked, 'What are you doing here, Mr Armstrong? I thought you were in the Navy.'

'I am, but I'm on sick leave. I got injured in the foot when I was on the ship.' He had their attention now and they both become very animated, asking him lots of questions about his ship. Ken asked if he had killed any Germans.

'Let Alan eat his breakfast, boys, please. And get on with yours as I want to talk to you before you go to school.'

Breakfast over, and with all four children in the kitchen, Jean addressed them all.

'You know that Daddy has died and gone to heaven and we haven't got a man to look after us.' She waited while they took this in and nodded. Alan stood quietly in a corner, admiring Jean. He was interested to see how she was going to broach the subject. He did not have long to wait. 'Well Alan, Mr Armstrong, has asked me to marry him and he is going to look after us all.' She smiled across at Alan who returned her smile then looked anxiously at the children.

An age seemed to go by before any of them spoke, but then Jeff, being the eldest, said, 'Does that mean you'll be living here with us?' As the question was directed at Alan he answered it. 'It would mean that usually, but you will all be coming to live with me in my house if you'd like that.'

Jean was anxious that things weren't going the way she'd expected.

'Will that mean you'll be our new daddy, Mr Armstrong?' Jeff asked.

'Not exactly. No one can take the place of your real Daddy, but I will be there for you and be as much like a Daddy as I can. And I will look after you and your Mummy and protect you all.'

'Have you got to go back to the Navy?' Ken asked.

'I don't think so Ken. You see, this wound I have on my foot, when it gets better I might walk with a limp, and the Navy might not allow me to return to the war. So I will be invalided out and that will mean I'll be at home all the time. But I won't be sure of that until I go for a medical board next week.'

Jean did not know this and it came as a bit of surprise. But secretly she was pleased.

'Will Michael be able to come and play with us at your house?' asked Jeff.

'Yes, of course he will, and any of your friends. And it won't be my house, but our house. If you like we can all go down to the house tomorrow and have a look at it. Then you can choose which bedroom you want.'

'You mean we won't all be in the same room?' Jeff asked.

'That's right.' With this Jeff got down from the table and went out the back door, calling out to Michael.

'Michael, Michael!' Michael came out to the back yard and Florrie came with him to see what all the noise was about.

'Michael, guess what! I'm getting a new daddy!'

'Cor! Who is it?'

Jean and Alan came out to the yard smiling at the way Jeff had accepted Alan. Alan had his arm loosely over Jean's shoulder.

'Mr Armstrong it is. And he said you can come and play with us at his house.' Jeff carried on chatting to Michael and Florrie took the opportunity to hug Jean, then Alan, and say, 'At last you have made your mind up. About time too. Can I be your bridesmaid?'

'Oh Florrie, of course you can,' said Jean laughing and crying at the same time.

Philip chose that moment to start yelling. Alan went to him and picked him up and Philip immediately stopped when Alan said to him, 'Come to Daddy.'

Ken and Janet had not taken much of a part in the drama that was unfolding about them until Janet went up to Alan and pulled his trouser leg for attention. Having got his full attention she said, 'Are you my Daddy too?'

He looked down at her and smiled. 'If you want me to be.'

Ken, not wanting to be left out asked, 'Me too?'

'Yes, of course you too. All of you,' he said, struggling to stoop down with Philip in his arms. Jean took Philip from him as he cuddled Ken and Janet. Even Jeff and Michael came over for a hug.

By now Jean and Florrie were both crying with joy and happiness. They were all stooped down crying and laughing and hugging in the back yard when a male voice came from behind them and demanded, 'What's all this row about? You've woken the whole neighbourhood.'

They all looked up to see Joe grinning down at them. Florrie leapt up and kissed him. 'I wasn't expecting you home today, dear. But we are all pleased to see you,' said Florrie.

They were standing up and Joe noticed that Alan was in the middle of all the excitement. Alan was still struggling to stand when Joe saluted him. 'Come off it, Joe. None of that here!' he protested, although he returned Joe's salute.

'What is all the noise about?' Joe asked again.

Jean answered him. 'Alan has asked me to marry him and it looks as though the children have accepted him for me,' she laughed, wiping her tears away.

'Yes, Joe,' said Alan smiling at him, 'and if you will do me the honour of being my best man, Jean and I will be very pleased.'

'Alan, I would love to be your best man. When is the happy day to be?'

'We haven't decided, yet,' Alan said smiling at Jean over the children's head.

'As far as I'm concerned the sooner the better,' Jean said. 'Come on everyone. It's school time for you boys.'

'Oh no, Mum. Can't we have a day off?' asked Jeff.

'Why not, Jean? Then we can all go up to my house and see what you think of it.'

'Please Mummy!' the boys demanded. Jean looked across at Alan, who was smiling lovingly at her. Jean could not resist his smile, so she said, 'Yes. All right then. But it's back to school on Monday.'

'Florrie, what about the job? I've just remembered. What am I going to do? It's my turn this morning,'

'Don't worry about it. I'll go in this morning and give notice while you and the children go up to see Alan's house.'

'Oh Florrie,' said Jean hugging her, 'I'll go in tomorrow.'

'No you won't. I'll work the notice out. Now scoot and get yourselves ready to see Alan's house.'

'Great!' shouted everyone.

Chapter Twenty-Two

Florrie went to work and Joe took Michael to school whilst Jean and Alan got Jean's children ready to go down to see Alan's house. Michael was very disappointed that he had to go to school when Jeff and Ken were going off with Mr Armstrong and Aunty Jean; he wanted to go too.

Between them, Jean and Alan managed to get the children ready by nine thirty.

'Will you be able to walk as far as Thames Ditton on crutches?' Jean asked of Alan.

'I should think so, at least as long as I take it easy. The doctors have told me that exercise is good for me, so it should be all right.'

They set off at a slow pace. Philip was in the pram with Janet sitting on the back of it, and Jeff and Ken each held on to the side of the pram. When they passed the Perspex factory a few of Alan's old workmates were coming out for a smoke break, so he stopped and had a word with them. Jean waited patiently for him to finish talking to them before they moved on towards the bridge.

'When are you going to tell your mother about us getting married Alan?'

'I've been wondering about that. What do you think of us going up there this afternoon?'

'Not much. I think you should be on your own when you break it to her,' Jean suggested.

'Yes, I think that's the best idea. I'll do that this afternoon and then and come straight round to tell you how it
went.'

'I expect it will come as a bit of a shock to her, especially
me having four children.'

'Ah, but you are forgetting that one of them is mine,
Jean. And don't forget that Philip is her first grandson as
well.'

Jean laughed and said, 'No I haven't! How on earth do
you expect me to forget that about Philip?'

Jean was thoughtful for a few minutes, then she turned
to Alan and said, 'Are you sure you want to go through with
this Alan? It's not too late to back down.'

'What's wrong, Jean. Cold feet?'

'No of course not. But I am still worried about you
taking on all of us, when only Philip is yours.'

'Jean, I love you and everything to do with you, and that
includes Jeff, Ken and Janet. So I don't want to hear any
more about me taking on too much. I am taking you all on
because I love you, warts and all.'

She burst out laughing and said, 'Mr Armstrong! Are
you calling my little darlings "warts"?'

Alan laughed too. 'You know I'm not, you fool.'

'Now I'm a fool!' Jean was still laughing when they
bumped into Mrs Mitchell.

'Hello Jean. Hello Alan. Nice to see everyone so happy.'

'Hello Mrs Mitchell,' they both said. 'You are looking as
beautiful as ever,' Alan continued.

'Alan Armstrong! Don't you give me any of your sailor-
boy flattery,' she laughed. 'I must say that I am glad you
two are getting together at last.'

'How did you know?' they both said at once, looking
quite guilty.

Mrs Mitchell laughed and said, 'I think the whole of Long Ditton must know, as you made enough noise about it in the back yard.'

Jean blushed saying, 'I am sorry, Mrs Mitchell, I hope we didn't disturb you.'

'No of course not. I am just pleased that you are both so happy and everything has turned out for the best. Things must have been bad since Tom died.'

'Yes. They have been. But one has to carry on.'

The children were getting a bit restless so Jean and Alan made their excuses, but Jean added as they were moving off, 'You will come to the wedding when we have decided on a day, won't you?'

Mrs Mitchell gave Jean and Alan a hug saying, 'You try and stop me. I'll be delighted to. Now you all get along with what you are doing and I'll see you later. Toodle-oo!'

'Goodbye Mrs Mitchell,' they both said.

'I thought you hadn't told anyone about Tom's death,' Alan said.

'I've told only the closest people I know, like Mrs Mitchell and the immediate neighbours. Only those I felt needed to know; apart from them, I don't think it's anyone else's business.'

'Oh, I see. That's fair enough. Now come on all of you. Chop, chop, and let's get this show on the road.'

They carried on toward Thames Ditton, a few people greeting them along the way. But they didn't stop to speak to any of them and only said hello in passing.

Soon Alan stopped in front of a large house and said, 'This is it.' Turning to Jean he asked, 'What do you think of it?'

Jean had always been impressed with this house, and had admired it every time she had passed it. 'I didn't know this was your house, Alan. I've always thought it lovely.'

'Well, now you're going to live in it.'

'Is this all yours, Mr Armstrong?' asked Jeff.

'Yes. Come on and see the rest of it,' he said walking up the path.

'Has it got a big back yard too?' Ken asked, not to be outdone.

'I'll tell you what. Why don't you all go around and see the back yard. It's just through that gate, and I'll take your Mummy to see the house. We'll meet you out there later.'

'All right, Mr Armstrong,' said Jeff, taking the pram from Jean and pushing it through the side gate.

Alan and Jean heard Jeff and Ken exclaiming and saying, 'Wow! This is great.'

'This I must see,' said Jean starting toward the side gate too.

Alan grabbed her arm saying, 'There is plenty of time to see the garden. Come on in and see the house. The children will be safe round the back.' With that he unlocked the front door and stood back to let Jean enter.

Jean entered and just stood in the hall looking around her. There were a lot of doors off the hallway, which was plushly carpeted in a dark red and black, with a lovely pattern of camellias on it in various colours. It was all oak panelled and had many oil paintings on the walls, set off by a lovely central staircase up to the first floor. This was oak too, and Jean thought it very graceful. The hall, despite being oak, was very light; it was lit by panels of glass on either side of the front door, and a large, beautiful arched stained glass window at the top of stairs. To top it all was a lovely crystal chandelier, its crystals making rainbow patterns over the furniture and walls where the sun shone through them.

Jean stood transfixed, her mouth open in wonder. Alan put his arms about her from behind and kissed the back of her neck. 'Nothing to say, Mrs Drummond?'

'Wow! as Jeff and Ken would say. If the hall is anything to go by, the rest must be beautiful.'

'My mother did the decorating throughout. But if there is anything you don't like, please feel free to change anything.'

Alan was pleased that she liked what she had seen already, and so had no hesitation in showing her the rest of the house. He led her through the first door on the left. This was a lounge with beautiful carpets, and the furniture covered in light-coloured floral chintz. There were pictures on the wall, and a scattering of delicate dark oak side tables. Jean turned to Alan bright-eyed and nearly in tears and said, 'It's so beautiful Alan. The kids won't be allowed in here, that's for sure.'

Alan laughed and said, 'I'm so pleased that you like it, Jean. There's a room at the back of the house that can be their play room.'

'I can't understand why your mother doesn't still live here instead of that tiny cottage down Windmill Lane. Who could leave somewhere as beautiful as this?'

'Obviously my mother. It is all due to memories. Memories of being so happy living here with my father, so much so that when he was dying she got him to change his will, leaving the house to me. She couldn't bear to live here after he died. He did change his will, and that is why the house is mine now. Anyway, Mother is very happy living in her cottage down the lane. She has her garden and her friends nearby. And she doesn't want for anything as my father left her very comfortably off.'

'How sad.' This time Jean cried.

'Oh, don't cry, Jean. She's very happy there. Come and see the rest of it.'

There was library off to the left, obviously where Alan spent most of his time. It had rows and rows of books from floor to ceiling, and some comfortable, but worn, leather chairs, and a desk with some papers on it.

'I can see this is where you spend most of your time when you are here, Alan,' murmured Jean.

'Yes it is.'

There were two other rooms at the front of the house, a formal dining room and another lounge. This one was less formal than the other one and looked more cosy. This, Jean decided, was going to be their family room.

At the back of the house was a huge kitchen. When Jean saw it she couldn't help exclaiming, 'Good Heavens Alan, this is as big as the whole of the downstairs at the cottage! With that big kitchen table the children will be able to have their meals out here.'

'That won't be necessary. Come here.' He led Jean through a door off the kitchen, and there overlooking the garden was a delightful sunny breakfast room which will be ideal for them to use as a family dining room.

'What a lovely little room! This will be just right for us to eat in,' said Jean. She looked out the window at the garden and watched the children for a while. They were playing on an old swing. There were trees at the bottom of the garden and the garden was laid to lawn with flower beds at the sides.

Ken looked up from watching Jeff push Janet on the swing and waved to her. She waved back and Ken turned away as it was his turn on the swing.

'I'll have to overhaul that swing as it's been there for years. I used to play on it when I was a kid. One of them could have an accident. Come upstairs and I'll show you the bathrooms and bedrooms.'

'Bathrooms!' exclaimed Jean. 'How many are there?'

'Three, would you believe. And a cloakroom with a toilet in it downstairs. All the bathrooms have toilets in them.' He looked a bit guilty as he showed Jean the opulence of the house considering what she was used to.

When he showed her the master bedroom she couldn't help herself and flung herself at Alan with more tears in her eyes. He drew her into his arms and kissed her and said, 'Oh Jean, Jean. I often pictured you here in this room.'

Jean pulled away, laughing, 'You dirty old man, Alan Armstrong!'

He laughed too, saying, 'No, I didn't mean like that Jean.'

'I'll bet!' she laughed.

'What I meant to say was in this house in general, not just in this bedroom but the whole house. Honest Jean.' She just laughed and wandered over to a door in the corner and opened it to find a bathroom there. 'Is this one of the three, or an extra one?'

'No. It's just one of the three,' he laughed.

Jean looked at the huge bed then at Alan. She saw the gleam in his eyes as he started to reach for her, but she managed to sidestep him and said, 'Don't you dare! I am not letting you near me that way until after we are married.'

Alan just burst out laughing at her and she said, 'I am serious about this. Not until after.'

He realised she was serious so agreed reluctantly but asked her for a kiss. Jean said that she would kiss him only if it wasn't in a room with a bed in it.

'Prude,' he muttered.

'I heard that, but I'll let it go this time.' Jean was hugging herself with happiness when she turned to Alan and said, 'I know we are all going to be very happy here Alan. Thank you.'

'My pleasure, Jean. Now let's go and look at the garden.'

As they opened the back door from the kitchen they heard Janet yelling with pleasure as she went flying off the swing and landed on the compost heap. She was laughing with joy. Jean and Alan rushed over to her, Alan surprisingly fast considering his disability. They both asked if she was all right but all they could get from her was laughter as she picked herself up and went back to the swing which had just broken.

'I give up,' Jean said laughing.

'That has decided me. I am going to fix that swing before anyone hurts themselves. Come on everyone,' Alan called to the children. 'Let's go and see who's having what bedroom.'

'You, young lady, are coming to the house so that I can clean you up before going home,' Jean said to Janet.

'Oh no Mum! I don't want to go home yet.'

'Alan, will be it okay to use the downstairs cloakroom to clean up this little ragamuffin?' Jean asked.

Alan was halfway up the stairs with the boys when Jean called, so he had to yell. 'Yes of course, you know where it is?'

'I think so. Thanks,' she yelled back. 'Now let's get you cleaned up.'

'Mummy, are we going to live in this big house?'

'Yes, darling. Did you hurt yourself when you fell from the swing?'

'No. It was good fun,' Janet laughed. 'What was that smelly stuff I landed in Mummy?'

'It's called a compost heap.'

'What's that?'

'That is where you put scraps of vegetable trimmings and leaves that have fallen from the trees, also grass cuttings.' Before Janet could ask why, Jean forestalled her and told her that it was then dug back in the garden when it had rotted enough, and that it made the soil better.

'Do you think it has rotted enough, Mummy?'

Jean laughed and said, 'If that smell is anything to go by I think it has.'

When Jean finished trying to clean up Janet and the mess she had made in the cloakroom she was ready to gather all the children together and take them home.

Alan was coming down the stairs rather gingerly as he still found stairs difficult to get down on the crutches. Jean was pleased to see Jeffery hanging on to Alan's uniform jacket to steady him.

When they were at the bottom of the stairs Alan turned to Jeff and thanked him for his help. Jeff smiled and blushed, and puffed out his little chest with pride.

Jean smiled and said, 'We had better get going as Mr Armstrong has to go to see his mother, so let's go and get the pram and start off home.'

Chapter Twenty-Three

Alan walked Jean and the children home and then went off to his mother's down Windmill lane. When Jean got indoors she went out the back to see Florrie and Joe.

'Come on, Jean! Tell me all about it,' said Florrie impatiently.

'Well, you know that house down Thames Ditton that we've always admired, well it's that one. Oh Florrie,' Jean said hugging her, 'I'm so happy. And the house is out of this world. You will have to come and see it tomorrow.'

'Just try keeping me away. By the way, where is Alan?'

'He's gone round to tell his mother about us. Then he's coming round to tell me what she thinks of the idea of us marrying. I'm dreading it.'

'Don't worry about it. She is sure to agree with anything Alan wants. She thinks the sun shines out of his porthole.'

'Really, Florrie,' Jean laughed. 'How can you be so sure?'

'Don't forget I've lived here for years so I know her quite well. Don't worry yourself over it.'

Jean still looked doubtful when she looked at Florrie, and Florrie just smiled and said, 'Trust me.'

They went indoors and Jean put the kettle on to boil. Joe did not bother to come in as he had decided to have a snooze before Michael came home from school.

'I have just realised that you're not at work. What happened?'

'Mrs Taylor was very nice about you giving notice. I have as well.'

'What! I thought you liked the job.'

'No, not really. I only did it for you. Anyway, Mrs Taylor is going away for a couple of weeks. She has given us what she owes us, and a little bit extra for you as a wedding present, and she thanked us both for what we have done for her.'

'Oh Florrie, how nice of her.'

Jean and Florrie sat drinking tea and eating broken biscuits and Jean told Florrie all about the house and garden. She even told her about Janet falling off the swing into the compost heap. That made Florrie laugh. 'That reminds me. I must strip her off – she doesn't smell too nice. Janet,' she called, and Janet came trotting in. 'I have to strip those clothes off you as they smell, and I'll have to bathe you too.'

'Oh no, Mum! Is it Friday already?'

'No it isn't, but you smell too much.'

Jean proceeded to sort Janet out and all the while telling Florrie about the rooms in the house. She said that she could not wait to move in.

She finished bathing Janet and sent her out to the back yard to play, while she started to get some lunch ready for them all.

'You'll stay to lunch won't you Florrie?'

'No thanks. I have a pile of ironing to do. So I'll try and get that done before Joe wakes up.'

'Okay then. I'll see you later.'

Florrie went through the fence to her cottage and Jean started preparing lunch. She opened a large tin of baked beans, put them in a saucepan to warm up and cut some bread. She would have preferred some toast but she didn't have the luxury of an electric toaster, and the fire wasn't lit, so bread it would have to be. In the end she decided to put margarine on it for a treat instead of just the dry bread.

When it was ready she called the children in. They came, and when they saw it was baked beans on bread they all cheered. It is funny that such a simple meal could bring so much pleasure, Jean thought. She preferred beans on toast herself but for now she was quite happy with the bread instead. In fact she was getting a bit nervous. She hoped Alan would be back soon.

The children were in the back yard playing and she was washing up the lunch things when Alan arrived. He sat down wearily in the armchair and removed his shoe and started to massage his bad foot. Jean dried her hands on a towel and went to him.

'Here, let me do that. You must be tired with all that walking.' She was dying to hear what had happened with his mother but she bided her time. She knew Alan would tell her soon.

'Everything is fine Jean,' Alan said, smiling at her.

'You mean she didn't object at all?'

'Oh, she did at first. Then when I told her that one of your children is mine she became more accepting; after all, she has no other grandchildren. She has invited you and the children to tea and I'm sure she will eventually grow to love you all.'

'Are you sure?'

'Yes of course I am. So I accepted on your behalf for tea tomorrow afternoon.'

'So soon?'

Alan was smiling when he answered her, 'Yes. So soon. Now give me a kiss then tell me what you want to alter in the house.'

Obediently she kissed him. It went on for quite a while until Jean pulled away and continued to massage his foot. 'There's nothing I want altering around the house. Perhaps I'll shift some furniture around, but that's all, although I would like to have the compost heap moved out of sight.'

'Is that all?' said Alan, relieved that that was all she wanted. Laughing he said, 'Did you manage to get Janet cleaned up all right?'

Jean laughed too. 'I even managed to get her in the bath. It is a pity I didn't put all the children in the bath. I didn't know we were going to meet your mother then. I'll do it in the morning before I take Florrie round to see the house. Will that be all right Alan?'

'Yes of course it is, silly.' He leaned over and kissed the top of her head adding, 'I tell you what, don't bath the children here, do it at the house. You won't have to lug the bath in or put the copper on for it, will you?'

'No, that's true.' Jean hugged herself and said, 'A real bath. What a luxury that will be, never to have to mess around boiling the copper up and lugging that bath in. Oh, and not having to use that outside loo ever again. I can't wait until we're married, Alan.'

'I see. You are only marrying me for my plumbing,' he laughed.

'No I am not. Now who's being silly?'

Jean and Alan took Florrie to see the house the following morning. They also took the children which meant another day off school for the boys. Jean was worried in case the School Board Inspector came to see her. Alan told her not to worry about it as it was only two days, and that she could write a note for Jeff to take with him when he and Ken went back to school on Monday.

Florrie loved the house and wandered around while Jean bathed the children. Even Janet said she wanted another bath. It must have been the novelty of it all.

When she had finished bathing the children she ran some fresh water for herself, although she felt guilty about it. Alan offered to scrub her back but she declined as Florrie was there.

★

Much to Jean's surprise, the dreaded visit to Alan's mother went very well.

Mrs Armstrong was a very pretty, petite and demure lady.

She asked Jean to sit beside her on the settee, and the older children on the other settee. Jean was thankful that they were behaving themselves. She could always count on Jeff and Ken, but she was not so sure about Janet. So she kept an eye on her.

All went well until they sat down to tea and Janet asked Jean, 'Mummy what is that thing next to the teapot?'

Jean looked and said, 'A sugar bowl dear.'

'No. The other thing.'

'Oh. It's a milk jug. Now sssh.'

'We usually have a bottle on the table,' she told the room proudly.

Alan just burst out laughing at that. Jean was mortified, but Mrs Armstrong was not put out by what Janet had said and just gave a little chuckle. Even Jeff and Ken were tittering. Jean could have murdered Janet for showing her up like that.

After that little episode was over, they all settled down to eat the beautiful spread that Mrs Armstrong had put on for them.

Tea finally over, with no more faux pas by the children – for which Jean was very thankful – Mrs Armstrong told the three older children that they could go out and play in the garden.

This was the dreaded moment, the tête-à-tête with Mrs Armstrong.

'When are you two planning on getting married?' she asked, not looking up from Philip, who was sitting quietly on her lap. She appeared to be besotted with him. Earlier when she had picked him up she had commented on his lovely blue eyes being just like Jean's.

Finally Alan said, 'As soon as possible. I have to go up to London for a medical to assess my disability on Monday, and depending on what they say we'll decide then.' He looked over and smiled at Jean who smiled back at him.

Mrs Armstrong saw this exchange and also the love they had for each other.

'Jean – may I call you that?'

'Yes of course. I'd be very pleased if you would.'

'Good. I want to say to you that I was a bit worried at first when Alan told me about you and the children. But I can see that they are beautifully behaved, and you have done a fine job bringing them up practically alone, Jean.'

'Thank you,' she said, blushing, and then added, 'I'm afraid that Janet is rather precocious and a bit too lively at times.'

Mrs Armstrong gave a delightful chuckle and said, 'She reminds me of when I was a little girl.'

'Mother! I didn't know you were like that as a little girl.'

'Lord yes! I was quite a tomboy too,' Mrs Armstrong said chuckling again.

They continued chatting for a while until Jean said reluctantly, 'Excuse me, Mrs Armstrong, but I feel it is time I took the children home.'

'So soon?'

'Well, it is nearly six o'clock, and it's time for Philip to be in bed. I'll get the children from the garden if that's all right with you Mrs Armstrong.'

'Yes of course, if you are sure you must go.'

Jean collected the children from the garden and they all thanked Alan's mother for a very nice tea.

As Jean was halfway through the front gate, Mrs Armstrong asked Jean if she would like to bring Philip and Janet round on Monday while Alan was in town and the boys at school.

'Thank you Mrs Armstrong. That would be nice.'

They arranged a time between them and Alan walked Jean and the children home. When they were well away from the cottage Alan said to Jean, 'There. That wasn't too bad was it?'

'No it wasn't. Your mother's a real sweetie!'

Chapter Twenty-Four

Jean sat in the armchair in the kitchen awaiting Alan's return from London. She had spent a very pleasant afternoon with Alan's mother, who had made a fuss of both children. Jean was pleased that Janet had behaved herself and hadn't say anything too outrageous.

The two women had talked and talked, about anything and everything. It seemed as though they had known each other for years rather than a few days.

Mrs Armstrong asked Jean about her mother. Jean told her that she had died not long before Jeff was born. Mrs Armstrong expressed the appropriate sympathy then astounded Jean by saying, 'You must let me do the reception for you, Jean.'

'No, I couldn't let you do that, Mrs Armstrong, although that is a very kind offer.'

'I insist, and won't take no for an answer. And if it is all right with you and Alan, I would like to have the reception here. Please let me do this, Jean,' she almost pleaded. Almost, but not quite.

Jean did not have the heart to refuse her. 'Well. All I can say is that would be a wonderful thing for you to do for us. I must admit that I hadn't thought that far ahead. So thank you very much.' With that, the two women hugged. They carried on chatting for a while until Jean said, 'I have to go and pick up the boys from school now. Thank you for a very pleasant afternoon,' and got up from the settee. Mrs Armstrong also got up and went and got their coats.

Jean thanked her again and gave her a peck on the cheek. 'I'll see you soon. Goodbye.'

'Goodbye Jean. Goodbye Janet.' She kissed Philip on his head and put him in the pram then waved to them until they were well up Windmill Lane.

Jean was still thinking of the afternoon when Alan arrived. They kissed and Alan sat down in the other armchair and sighed. 'I'm worn out. But seeing you makes me forget how tired I am. So come here and give me another kiss and tell me what sort of day you have had.'

She kissed him and then sat at his feet and asked him how his medical went.

'It went quite well really. Physically they passed me one hundred per cent fit apart from my foot. But because of the foot I am now classed as unfit for sea duties.'

He added that although he was not fit enough to go to sea he would be pushing a pen in an office in London.

She reached up and kissed him again and asked him, 'Are you terribly disappointed?'

'I am a bit, because I enjoyed the action at sea and the life on board. But it will now mean I will be able to get home most nights to see you and the children.'

'Where are you being posted?'

'The Admiralty.'

'That will be lovely. Perhaps I will be able to persuade Florrie to babysit at the house so I could snatch a day or two in town.'

'I am glad you brought that up as I was going to suggest something like that for when we get married.'

'What do you mean?'

'Babysit for a few days so that I can take you for a couple of days' honeymoon.'

'Oh, Alan! I never thought of that. I didn't have a honeymoon with Tom, you see. We couldn't afford one.' Her eyes misted over with the thought of Tom. Alan noticed this and pulled her onto his lap and cuddled her. She kissed him and said that a honeymoon would be a lovely idea.

'Where shall we go, Alan?'

'Anywhere you want to go.'

'I don't know where to go.'

'I'll tell you what, why not just get in the car and go down to the West Country?'

'Don't be daft. You haven't got a car, Alan.'

'Oh yes I have. That was why I was later getting back than planned. I bumped into an old friend that I knew at university. He had this car for sale that was much too big for his needs now, so I made him an offer and he accepted. It's parked out the back by the coal merchants.'

'That's wonderful. Will you have enough petrol vouchers for the petrol to take us to the West Country?'

'I think so. It is nearly full now and I will be able to get some more on the way. Now tell me, how did you get on with my mother this afternoon?'

'Really well. It felt as though I've known her for ages. And guess what?'

'What.'

'She has insisted on organising the wedding reception for us at her cottage. Isn't that nice of her?'

'Yes it is. Now then. When shall we get married? I have a month before I take up my new job in London. That's when the doctors think my foot will be fully healed. So when?'

'How about tomorrow?' Jean laughed knowing full well that they could not organise it by then.

'We'll have to wait until tomorrow to find out when Joe will be able to get time off from the RAF. If my mother is doing the reception we'll have to give her notice as she will need time to fix everything for it.'

Jean gave Alan a lingering kiss and he started to run his hand up and down her leg. She pushed his hand away and said, 'None of that until after we are married.'

'You're not still sticking to that plan, are you Jean?'

'Yes I am. But you are welcome to stay here tonight though. You can sleep downstairs and I will sleep upstairs.'

'Oh Jean! What does it matter now whether I stay or not? Or if we make love or not?'

'I don't know really. It's just a feeling I have that I have to do things properly. Call me old-fashioned if you like, but that is how I feel.'

'In that case the sooner we get married the better my love. I'll start sorting things out tomorrow.'

Jean kissed him again and he said, 'Stop teasing me like that if you don't want me to take you right here and now.'

'Don't you dare, Alan Armstrong!' she said, struggling to get out of his arms. But he was too strong for her and he had her tightly trapped in his arms.

Pulling back from him she said, 'I've heard that if it is inevitable, just lay back and enjoy it.'

'Hussy,' he said against her lips, 'now come here and let me make love to you.'

'No Alan. I mean it.' He kissed her again and she had no will-power to fight him.

'We had better get up to my bedroom then, or under the shelter.'

'The shelter is nearer, so come on.' Jean got up from his lap and they went to the front room.

★

In the morning, while Jean was cooking breakfast and Alan was playing in the front room with the children, Florrie put her head round the back door and asked if Jean was decent.

'Of course I am. Come in. The tea is made if you want a cup.'

'No thanks, but thanks all the same. I just came to see how things went yesterday.'

At that moment Alan came in from the front room.

'Good morning Florrie. I thought I heard you. How are you?'

'Fine thanks Alan. And you?'

'Very well thanks. Is Joe still here? I want to have a word with him later.'

'Yes, he's just finishing off his breakfast. Do you want me to give him a message?'

'No that's all right. Tell you what. What are the three of you doing this afternoon?'

'Nothing that I know of. Why?'

'I want to ask Joe when he will be home next regarding our wedding. So I was thinking, why don't we all go down to that pub in Thames Ditton, The White Swan, and have a pub lunch. It'll be my treat. What do you say to that?'

'That would be lovely Alan. Thank you. I'll tell Joe. Won't that be too far for you to walk though?'

'I don't think so. If I do find it too much I can always stop at the house for a rest. Or Jean can let me sit on the pram instead of Janet,' he laughed.

'Your breakfast is ready Alan. Are you sure you won't stay for a cuppa, Florrie?'

'No, but thanks all the same. I only came over to see how Alan got on at the medical. He can tell us later when we are down the pub. See you later.' With that she was gone before they could say goodbye.

They all spent a pleasant few hours down at the riverside pub. There was a garden for the children to play in so the adults did not have to keep an eye on them. Michael and Jeff were in charge of the younger children and took the responsibility seriously. Jean and Alan and Florrie and Joe were able to get down to organising the wedding. Joe would be home again in two weekend's time. That was when they decided to get married, but to do it they would need to get a special licence.

Joe asked if they would like another drink. They all said yes and he went up to get them: a pint each of bitter for Alan and Joe, and sweet sherries for Jean and Florrie.

When Joe sat down he took a sip of his pint and said that he would like to propose a toast. 'Here's to the future bride and groom. May you have much happiness and a long and fruitful marriage.'

Alan and Jean thanked Joe for the good wishes and they all tapped their glasses together. Joe said that he was just getting some practice in for the big day.

Chapter Twenty-Five

The big day was nearly upon them. Jean had finished making the suit she was going to wear only two days before the wedding. Alan would wear his naval uniform, which pleased Jean, as he looked very handsome in it.

Jean's father and her brother Len were coming to the wedding. She was very pleased that her father could come, as he would be able to give her away. Florrie and Len would act as witnesses and sign the Register. Her other brother and his wife could not make it but sent their best wishes.

Alan had made all the wedding arrangements. The ceremony was to be at the registry office in Kingston and the wedding breakfast at Alan's mother's. The wedding was at one o'clock, giving people time to get there if they were coming from a distance.

Jean had felt guilty that she had not had to organise anything herself for the wedding. Alan and his mother had done everything, bless them. All she had done was make her suit and a pretty frock for Janet.

The car that Alan had bought came in very handy taking things from Jean's cottage round to the house. She would not need any of the furniture that was in the cottage, as the house had everything she needed in it. The only thing she would need there was her sewing machine, and now she had finished her suit Alan could take it round to the house. Apart from that there would only be the children's things, her clothes, a few bits and pieces that had been her mother's, and a couple of keepsakes.

'How about taking the Morrison shelter Jean?' Alan said laughingly.

She laughed too and said that it was not such a bad idea at that.

He looked longingly at it and said, 'Come on Jean. One last time on it here.'

'I am not going to bed with you now until after the wedding. That's only the day after tomorrow. But that's a good idea about taking it round to the house. I still haven't changed my mind about going down an air-raid shelter you know.'

'All right Jean. I'll make arrangements for it to be picked up and taken round the house before we get back from our honeymoon. Now come on. Just one more time, darling.'

'No, Alan! You are a sex maniac,' she laughed. 'I have told you not until after we are married. Please. Surely you can wait one day?'

'It's two nights Jean. But if you insist I had better get off home. I'll be round to pick up those boxes of toys of the children's tomorrow morning, Jean.' He stood up and kissed her longingly. 'Are you sure?'

'Yes I am,' she said, pushing him from her and laughing. 'Now go home. I'll see you for breakfast in the morning.'

'All right spoilsport. I'll see you in the morning. Good-night Jean.'

'Goodnight Alan.'

She shut the door after him and cleared away the plates they had used for supper and went up to bed.

She was too excited to sleep, going over and over in her mind how she wanted the furniture moved in the house. She would have the luxury of a sewing room just off the library.

Florrie had been a lot of help to her, helping pack boxes and suitcases, taking things down to the house using the pram when Alan was off doing other things in the car.

Eventually she slept.

★

The day of the wedding dawned bright and clear with just a light breeze. The children were getting overexcited so Florrie took them off Jean's hands for a walk over the Rec. That left Jean to pack her suitcase for the honeymoon.

She looked down at her left hand and at the ring Alan had given her the previous evening. It was a beautiful ring with a huge blue sapphire surrounded by diamonds. He said it was antique and had belonged to his grandmother on his mother's side. Alan's mother had given it to him on Thursday for Jean. His mother did not wear it herself as she preferred the one that Alan's father had bought her. Jean took Tom's rings from her left hand and put them on her right.

'Oh Alan! It's so beautiful.' Jean was nearly in tears.

'Mother said that it would match your eyes. And it does.'

She finished packing and went to make all the beds and leave the place tidy. Florrie was going to pack up the rest of the things when Jean and Alan were away. The bulky items Jean and Alan would decide what to do with when they came back from their honeymoon.

Alan had arranged to pick Jean and the children up at twelve fifteen, so Jean started to get ready. By the time she had nearly finished, Florrie was back with the children.

Both Jean and Florrie got the children washed and dressed. Fortunately they had not got too dirty since they had had a bath the day before, so there was not much to wash off. They helped them into their best clothes and did the boys' ties up, dressed Janet in her new frock and warned them not to go out into the back yard.

She thanked Florrie for her help and went to finish off dressing. She was wearing her dressing gown over her undies and slip. She took out a brand new pair of nylons from their packet and carefully put them on. Alan had got a few pairs when he was up in London last week. She did not ask how he had got them. 'The sheer luxury of them,' she thought. 'Makes a change from the lisle ones I am used to. Or none at all.' She had given Florrie a pair so that she could wear them to the wedding too.

All ready, they were waiting for Alan. He was right on time. Alan said that Jean looked beautiful and the boys looked very handsome in their matching suits and smart ties. Even Janet looked pretty in her new dress.

They arrived at the Registry Office in Kingston in plenty of time. Jean was pleased to see that her father and Len had arrived. She introduced them to Alan and his mother. There were some friends of Alan's who were introduced to Jean. Mrs Mitchell with a couple of the neighbours had also arrived.

Having decided that everyone was there Joe ushered them all inside the Registry Office.

Just before going in Jean took off the wedding and engagement ring that Tom had given her, and put Alan's engagement ring on her other hand. She handed Tom's rings to Florrie, and said, 'I'll keep these for Janet. Will you hold on to them until after the ceremony, please?' Although she had taken them off reluctantly she knew it was the beginning of a new life for them all.